# DEBUNKED

## BETH PERRY

**World Castle Publishing, LLC**
Pensacola, Florida
Copyright © 2024 Beth Perry
Paperback ISBN: 9798891261600
eBook ISBN: 9798891261617
First Edition World Castle Publishing, LLC, March 5, 2024
http://www.worldcastlepublishing.com
**Licensing Notes**
Cover: Cover Designs by Karen
Cover-Designs-by-Karen.com
Editor: Karen Fuller

My gratitude goes out to friend and author Betty Ann Harris for allowing me to borrow her lovely name.

For Evelyn and Autumn.

# CHAPTER ONE

It was a humid third Thursday in July, and Craig Herbert was still a little stiff from plane travel. Except for three layovers during his trip from LAX to the Tricities Airport in Blountville, the journey to Tennessee had been uneventful. Craig had fallen asleep during the last leg of the trip. It had taken a couple of cups of coffee at the Tailwind restaurant before the fog left his brain. From there, he took the brisk walk from baggage claims to the Airport Car Rentals. There, he had paid for a two-day rental on a Pacifica Hybrid and asked for directions to the Brook View Hotel. To his relief, the nice rental woman with the distinctive East Tennessean accent told him the hotel was conveniently located just across the highway. He drove there and was checked in by a middle-aged couple by the names of Josette and Lathan Ford.

The two were friendly but extremely chatty. As they ran his credit card, they told him they were the owners, having inherited it from Josette's parents, and that their son Frank would one day inherit it. Frank had two daughters. Daughter-in-law Beverly was expecting a baby in October. The couple's dog Rowdy usually minded the door, but he had died some months back. *Do you have a dog, sir? What's the weather like in California? You know, Uncle Francis used to live in Apple Valley, and he had a nice wife named Barbara. What brings you to Tennessee? Oh, you are an executive field producer for a television show? Why, cousin Andy met his first wife on some dating show out in Hollywood! That was back in the sixties, and Andy is dead now. The wife, oh, she was nice enough, though their boy ended up serving some years in prison for tax fraud.*

By the time Craig made the way to his room door, he guessed he knew half of the Fords' combined life stories.

Only after entering the room did it occur to him that despite their gift for gab, the couple was nothing like the kind of people he had feared East Tennesseans to be. The Fords were decent folks. Neither did they seem to be alone in this – no one at the airport or at the car rental place had treated him discourteously or in any way differently. He realized the expectation of finding the region filled with hostile rednecks who would hate him on the spot simply for being black had been without merit. He considered the possibility that at the age of twenty-six, he was just now learning the world, and the people in it weren't exactly what he'd been taught in college or the popular news networks. This realization was not one he was proud of. He imagined how disappointed his dad and mom would be by the presumption. His parents had taught him one couldn't afford to assume the worst about anyone –no matter what they looked like or where they came from. To do this, they had warned, only betrayed the worst about oneself.

Craig's schedule allowed little time to waste on self-chiding. He dumped his backpack of clothes on the bed, adjusted the air conditioning to a comfortable temperature, and set up his laptop on the desk in the room.

Less than fifteen minutes later, he was back inside the Pacifica to start the search for the person he'd come to see. He had never been to this part of Tennessee (only to Memphis a couple of times, years ago, to visit his maternal great-grandparents). He hoped the next stage of the journey didn't require him to travel too far from this semi-rural hub section of the Tricities. The idea of having to drive through Bristol, Johnson City, or Kingsport –all places Craig had barely heard of – was not an appealing prospect.

He owned a Hybrid Mini Cooper, which he'd left in Hancock Park for his sister Kesha to use. Kesha was a student nurse and did a lot of driving back and forth from classes as well as getting to her part-time waitress job. Craig much preferred taking a cab or hitching a ride with his peers for his trips between home and his studio office at the Awareness Television Network. Long drives were not his thing.

Now, after configuring the travel destination into his phone's GPS, the system's electronic voice informed him that Squirrel Hollow Road was approximately ten minutes away.

Craig had expected this part of the state to be as mountainous as the nearby Smokies. To his surprise, this area close to Blountville was more hilly than mountainous. The road he traveled took him past rolling pasture land and farm houses, little clusters of suburbs, and several fishing ponds. The GPS directed him to the community of Indian Springs. This was a pristinely picturesque area, dotted on either side of the road with beautiful old homes, churches, and the occasional small shopping center.

The electronic voice piped up with an alert the next right ahead would take him onto Squirrel Hollow Road.

It was a narrow road cut and paved through a section of rural land that lay between two very lengthy hills. There were many single-wide trailers to either side of the road, most all spaced apart by vegetable gardens or private tobacco allotments. At one point, he noticed to his right a timeworn log cabin-type church. There was no sign on either the property or the church itself to indicate what it was called, and the GPS system provided no address. Situated on the hillside between the church and the woodland was a cemetery. By the style of the thin slab headstones and the iron fencing surrounding the graves, Craig guessed the cemetery was as old as or older than the church.

The road brought him through a series of tight curves flanked by denser woodland. He passed by several driveways nearly hidden by the overgrowth. At last, the road straightened, and Craig found himself traveling between two lengthy lots of cleared property. He guessed this had been farm land at one point, though now there was no sign of agricultural use, barns, or livestock. As the road ascended slightly, he saw a two-way intersection just up ahead. To the left side of the road was a large pond surrounded by dense thickets, though again, no animals, no sign of commercial farming of any sort. To the right-side of the road, just before the intersection, lay an entrance way to a modern-looking brick building.

The GPS said in its monotone voice, "Take the next right for the Indian Springs Senior Citizens Center."

Craig slowed and turned into the entrance. Erected just inside stood a stone monument-type sign. The welcoming panel read in dark, verdant text, "Indian Springs Senior Citizens Center." Just past this was a large parking lot close to the brick building.

There were only a few other vehicles in the lot. As Craig took one of the spots, he noticed three elderly women standing and talking at a cement walkway which led behind the center.

Craig turned off the engine and picked up his phone. He found the last message exchange he'd had with Heather Schaffer. Heather was the guest scout for *The Debunkers Challenge* (and aside from his sister, the one person Craig felt close to). It was on Heather's recommendation that Craig had made the trip to Tennessee. This contact he was about to meet was actually Heather's great-uncle. Reading back through the messages, Craig saw the uncle's name was Fred Wagner. As Heather recalled, Uncle Fred was in his eighties now. Uncle

Fred claimed to have a good friend who was just right to be a guest on the show. Heather admitted she had not seen Uncle Fred in many years and had surprised herself when he'd called. Heather would have made the trip out to Tennessee in order to meet her uncle's friend, but she was stuck at home on maternity leave.

TDC was a popular series, and for the season's eighth and final episode, the guest scheduled to be challenged was Brenda Lindt. This Lindt was a proclaimed clairvoyant from Indiana. She professed to be able to talk to the dead and made a living from selling her talents to wealthy clients. Like other acclaimed clairvoyants, Lindt had increased her fame by penning a number of bestselling books. She'd also done the psychic circuit, doing arena shows where her loyal believers could meet her and hopefully get her to use her alleged abilities to help them. But three weeks earlier, Lindt had suffered a massive heart attack, and her appearance on the show had to be canceled. As field manager, Craig knew this cancellation threatened to put a crimp into the tight production schedule. There was also the show's creator and host of TDC to contend with. Gerald Agee was a psychic debunker by trade –having written prolifically on the subject with a legion of diehard blog followers—and not, to put it kindly, a modest or patient man by temperament.

Although Agee preferred going after the big-name cranks and frauds, none of Lindt's peers had shown interest in filling her slot. This was understandable, Craig conceded, as so many of their peers had been disgraced over the years by failing to meet the variety of challenges faced on TDC. Not even the juicy possibility of impressing the judges and claiming the prize of three million dollars was enticing enough to get any of them in front of a camera.

But Agee demanded Lindt's slot to be filled asap. So if that meant Craig had to book some psychic without national recognition or online presence, then so be it. Agee and the studio had till the following spring to sign-up better-known charlatans for the ninth season.

Craig read Heather's message: "You should recognize Uncle Fred by the fact he uses a wheelchair."

Glancing toward the Center, he thought wryly, *I'm likely to come across a dozen old men in wheelchairs in a place like this.*

Heather's message entry also informed him that the person Uncle Fred wanted him to meet was a woman named Betty Ann Crawford. Craig slipped the phone into the pocket of his shirt and, taking the car keys, stepped out. After locking the doors, he walked toward the center. As he reached the cement walkway out front, he saw a man in an electric wheelchair moving along the walkway from the back area. Doubting he would be lucky enough for this to be Uncle Fred, Craig walked forward to meet him.

He was a very clean-cut old gent with thinning snow-white hair. Craig guessed him to be in his late seventies. The man touched a button on the panel of the wheelchair's left arm rest. The chair came to a halt.

Before Craig could ask his name, the old guy regarded him with a pleasant look. "Might you be Mr. Craig Herbert?"

"Yes, sir, I am. You wouldn't happen to be Fred Wagoner?"

"I sure am, Mr. Herbert. She told me you'd arrived."

Remembering his manners, Craig extended his hand. Mr. Wagoner had a stronger shake than he would have guessed.

"Nice to meet you, sir. That's right, I left a message on Heather's phone when my plane arrived at the airport. I appreciate her letting you know."

A confused stitch cut across Mr. Wagoner's brow. Then he smiled. "Oh no, I didn't mean my niece. It was Betty Ann.

She just told me some moments ago I'd find you out front here."

Craig wondered how any of the women he'd noticed earlier could have seen him as he sat in the car? But he imagined this Betty Ann must have keen eyesight for her age.

"Ah yes, Miss Crawford – it is Ms. Crawford? Or does she prefer Betty Ann?"

"She goes by Betty Ann around here." Mr. Wagoner's face beamed tenderly. "How is our Heather? She told me that her baby is due quite soon."

"Heather is well," Craig assured him. "The baby is healthy, and yes, due in a couple of weeks, I believe. So, I should ask, does Betty Ann know why I'm here? I would hate for this to be an out-of-the-blue meeting for her."

Wagoner made a little grunt. "Oh, she knows. It was Betty Ann who asked me to get hold of Heather," Wagoner explained. "Apparently, she knows all about your television show. She asked me to contact Heather. Of course, I advised Betty Ann against having anything to do with that kind of television nonsense. No offense intended, Mr. Craig."

Craig let him know that no offense was taken. To make small talk, he remarked, "This is nice out here in the country. Peaceful. A good place for a Seniors Home."

"This is no *home*," Wagoner said. "Fancy name, maybe. But it's more like a club. I used to own a nice dairy over near the original Holston elementary school. But my sons moved away as they are apt to do, and when I got too old to run the farm, I sold it. I was born and raised here on Squirrel Hollow Road. Always loved it. So, with the boys gone, I moved back to my family's old property. I bought some other property, too, the lot here among it. And more recently, that open field across the road. I reckon you noticed the pond over there on your way here? It's all grown up and woody on the backside now."

Craig nodded and listened politely as Wagoner continued, "When I was a kid old Elmer Perkins owned most all this property. Perkins had inherited it, and as he was a bricklayer by trade, he didn't have much use for farming. So, every year, he'd lease it out. From early summer to the middle of fall, you'd find the PTA, the Four-H, the Shriners, and the livestock clubs holding their fundraisers and fairs and such. Passing carnivals, too. The carnival folk would set up across the road behind the pond. All that stopped when Perkins passed away. That was back in the early eighties, if I reckon right. In fact, when I bought this portion, I thought about leasing it out like Perkins used to. But then I got to thinking, I have lots of neighbors my age out here. Friends of the same age all round this area, too. And I figured it'd be a real nice place to have somewhere we could all meet up and socialize in our golden years."

Craig was impressed. "So you built this center?"

Wagoner nodded. "Yes." He looked at Craig thoughtfully and said in a no-nonsense way, "Mr. Herbert, everyone that regularly comes here is a person I consider my friend. The members, their families, the staff. And it wouldn't sit well with me to find out any of my friends had been disrespected."

Craig realized he'd just been given a diplomatic but firm warning by the old man. If it had been Gerald Agee who had received such a warning, Mr. Wagoner would have just been laughed at. But Craig valued civility. And the truth was he felt a twinge of remorse for coming here in the first place. He imagined how Wagoner's elderly friend Betty Ann would feel once she realized how decidedly out of her favor Agee's psychic challenges were designed. No one was supposed to impress Agee, his live audience, or his panel of *impartial* judges. Everything was constructed to disprove the integrity of the guests, to expose them as frauds, and to do so as humiliatingly as possible.

"I understand," Craig told Wagoner. "Of course."

"They are good people," Wagoner expounded. "You won't find riff-raff hanging around."

Craig found Wagoner's attitude admirable. TDC was in dire need of a slot fill, but if this Betty Ann Crawford was anything like Wagoner, Craig would have to find some excuse to book somebody else.

He assured Wagoner again that he understood. The old man seemed satisfied.

"So you want to interview our Betty Ann?" he said. "I think *interview* is the word Heather used."

"Yes, sir. You did tell Heather this lady is a medium?"

"I don't know if that's rightly the proper word, but once I told Heather about Betty Ann, she told me it fit." Wagoner gave a little disapproving sniff. "*Applicable for what Betty Ann claims to be*, that was what she said. But Betty Ann never claimed to be anything. I just know what she can do. So does everyone here at the Center. And I've caught a few episodes of your show myself since, after all, my niece works on it. *The Debunker's Challenge*, right?"

"Yes, sir."

"Uh-huh. So when Betty Ann brought it up, I thought to myself, who among use couldn't use three million dollars? If the show is legitimate, I can see her winning. And one would deserve taking home that kind of money more than her."

Craig was very conscious of the sun beating down on the top of his head. His scalp tickled with sweat, and for a moment, all he could think about was the desire for something cold to drink. But he stifled it. He hoped to inquire more into Betty Ann's alleged medium abilities before they were introduced.

"Mr. Wagoner, how did you meet Betty Ann?" he asked. "And can you tell me more about her powers as you have witnessed them yourself?"

Wagoner shrugged. "She came here some months ago. It was right after I bought the property across the road. A few days before Easter, it was. None of us had ever seen her before, but here she comes out back where we're all eating barbecue. She brought a huge platter of deviled eggs. We were missing deviled eggs at the barbecue, so everybody was real grateful to see them. And then we realized we were happy to see Betty Ann, too. Real sweet gal. She comes here practically every day now. She loves taking care of plants. She still brings deviled eggs every Sunday afternoon."

Craig smiled indulgently, but Wagoner wasn't telling him what he needed to know. "When did you and your friends realize she has other *talents*?"

"Mr. Herbert, I realized Betty Ann was special the day after she first showed up. I had misplaced my wedding band. Had been looking for it for over a week. Betty Ann came up to me and said I would find the ring in my backyard. It had slipped off, she told me, while I was pointing out to my grandson Justin where I wanted him to trim the hedges. When I got home, I asked Justin to help me look for it. The ring was there alright, in the grass next to the garage door."

Craig raised an eyebrow. He knew this story was one of pure coincidence. "Has Betty Ann personally advised or suggested help with any other problems?"

"In a way, I suppose you can say," Wagoner said. "That would have been about my neighbor Charlie Mayo. Charlie thinks he's too young to hang out here. But nice man. Works at the box factory in Johnson City. Anyway, yes, Betty Ann was real helpful for Charlie's son and his family."

Craig felt sweat trickling down the nape of his neck and inching slowly down the top of his spine. He reached to the back of his collar and pulled it away from his damp skin. With any hope, a little air would dry the sweat and relieve the temptation to yank his shirt off. He tried concentrating on what Wagoner had just said.

"What did Betty Ann do for Charlie's son and family, Mr. Wagoner?"

"Well, sir, Betty Ann was here that day. She was helping some of the other ladies plant Iris bulbs when she suddenly got up from her knees, where she kneeled on the grass. There was this look on Betty Ann's face –like something had her really worried. She came to me and begged that I call Charlie and tell him to call his son Dean right away. Dean just had to check on his little girl, she said. Now remember, she's never met Charlie, nor Dean and his wife, Frannie. But Betty Ann insisted Frannie was asleep and that their eight-month-old was locked in her car. So I called Charlie. Charlie called Dean. Dean was just getting off work when Charlie got through to him. The boy drove home and found the baby still in the car seat of his wife's car. The door was stuck somehow and couldn't be opened. Dean grabbed the tire iron from his trunk and broke the window to get to the baby. From what I've been told –and excuse me for repeating gossip — Frannie cares more about getting stoned than practically anything else. She was dead asleep in the air-conditioned house and had completely forgotten to take that little baby out of the car."

Craig winced. "Was the baby okay?"

Wagoner nodded. "Yes. But Frannie and Dean are separated now, and he's got the baby. I imagine that's for the best. But we all have Betty Ann to thank for Dean getting to the baby before something unthinkable happened."

This tale was indeed unsettling. And Craig was convinced now Betty Ann was more involved with the people Wagoner knew than the poor man suspected.

"So," Craig said as evenly as he could muster, "I have to admit, a story like this might lend one to wonder if Betty Ann doesn't possess some kind of sixth sense? Or perhaps

Betty Ann has known Frannie for some time?"

Wagoner gave him an incredulous look. "Are you serious, young man? Even if by some extraordinary coincidence the two have met, Frannie and Dean live all the way in Texas."

Craig was dubious, and now he asked more snidely than intended, "Seriously? This incident with the baby happened all the way down in Texas?"

The tone of his voice obviously annoyed Wagoner, for the old gent replied curtly. "*Seriously*, Mr. Herbert. All the way down in Texas."

Craig did not want to insinuate Heather's uncle was a liar. But there was no way a human being could be aware of a baby trapped inside a car from thousands of miles away. For all he really knew, the seemingly upstanding Fred Wagoner was just an old fibber, one who set up his niece on some lavish prank. The possibility also occurred to Craig that, more sadly, Heather's uncle was simply as deteriorated of mind as he was of body.

Wagoner gave a weary smile. "Look, I'll take you round back now to meet Betty Ann. It's hot out here. Shall I get our staff girl Emily to bring you a glass of cold lemonade? I noticed Ida Johnson had put a big old pitcher of it in the fridge this morning."

The offer was very appealing. "Thanks, that would be very welcome," Craig said. "Before we go, you should know I'd like to speak to any of your friends here who believe they've also been helped by Betty Ann's powers. And it would be useful if I could videotape what they have to say. Get your eyewitness account, too. If this is alright by everyone involved?"

"I prefer not sharing that particular story since it involves Charlie's family, and none of them are here for you to ask. But I can ask the others. I'm sure most of them would be agreeing." Wagoner pressed a button on the wheelchair panel, and it turned with a little *whirr* sound. Craig walked beside Mr. Wagoner as the wheelchair moved down the walkway. The motor of the chair produced a noticeable wheezing sound. Wagoner apologized.

"Motor is giving out," Wagoner said. "I need to replace this old contraption soon. Had this one almost twelve years now."

They followed the curve, which led them to the back part of the Center. Here, a lattice-iron gate opened to an ample, nicely maintained enclosure bordered by a meandering stone wall. Fragrant sweet peas trailed profusely up the side of the wall. In the middle of the lawn were three grown tulip poplars (presently in full bloom). Beneath the boughs stood two wooden picnic tables. A dozen or more seniors sat at the benches, engaged in conversation and playing cards or checkers. Plots of flowering plants had been arranged all about the edge of the Center's back patio. On this patio sat a very old woman in a wheelchair, and beside her was a slightly younger woman seated in a plastic lawn chair. Between the two women lay a roan-colored Labrador retriever that appeared to be sleeping.

Wagoner steered the wheelchair across the patio. Craig half-expected Wagoner to stop and introduce him to his friends, but the old man continued onto a short piece of walkway. As they walked along, Craig noticed a wall ahead and, before it, a thriving mass of dark pink roses. A woman knelt on the ground. Her back was to them, so Craig couldn't tell what kind of work she was doing. On approaching her, Wagoner stopped the wheelchair.

"Betty Ann," Wagoner said, "this is the gentleman from that debunkerin' TV show."

Craig watched as Betty Ann laid a small gardening spade on the ground. She rose to her feet and turned. He was surprised to see this was no elderly woman, not even one of middle years. She was quite young; Craig guessed somewhere between nineteen and twenty-five years of age.

He thought this Betty Ann was not hard on the eyes, either. Her skin was very fair, her face youthful, and her cheeks and nose sprinkled with golden freckles. Her eyes were a very light shade of blue, and her shoulder-length fair hair shone like gold in the sunlight, kissed here and there with sun-bleached streaks. From Betty Ann's wrist hung a homespun bracelet of elastic band threaded through seashell pasta. It was cute, something an elementary school child might make for their mother. There were sandals on her feet, adorned with rhinestone-beaded thong straps. The cut-off denim shorts she wore (slightly sullied by dirt) showed off her lovely long legs. Craig noticed, too, the black shirt she wore. It looked well-worn, and there was a somewhat faded image on the front. It took Craig a couple of moments to recognize the image as a spaceship. And only then did he realize the shirt was a classic *Boston* concert tee.

Craig decided this woman was not so much beautiful as she was fresh and naive in appearance.

*And appearances,* he remembered, *were often deceiving.*

Betty tilted her face ever so slightly and looked at him. Slowly, her lips spread into a timid smile. Craig was charmed by the touch of an overbite to her front teeth.

"Hello, Betty Ann," Craig said and extended his hand to shake hers. "Craig Herbert. You can call me Craig."

At last, she said to Mr. Wagoner, "Fred, would you ask Emily to bring Mr. Herbert one of the colas from the machine in the rec room? He'd prefer that over Ida's lemonade. She can be stingy on the sugar."

"Sure thing," Wagoner answered. He turned the wheelchair and headed to the patio. As it moved off Craig was hardly aware of the motor's wheeze. He was wondering if

Betty Ann had just guessed Wagoner and he had talked about Ida's lemonade. He didn't want to mention this, though. He would give no hint he could think she actually possessed the gift of foreknowledge.

He put on his most professional smile. "Is there a place we can sit down to talk?"

Betty Ann eyed the yard.

"There?" she suggested, pointing to a grassy place in the shade just a few feet away. Craig hoped they could just go inside for this interview, but as he opened his mouth to make the suggestion, Betty Ann walked into the yard and took a seat in the grass. She hugged her knees and gave him a patient look.

Craig felt awkward about sitting on the grass in perfectly clean and recently pressed clothes. And he was a grown man, here on business. He couldn't help but wonder what kind of childish country bumpkin this Betty Ann was not to take such things into consideration?

He looked at the seniors sitting at the tables and saw that only a couple of them even looked his way.

"Nobody cares if you do," he heard Betty Ann say.

He knew the clothes he wore weren't his best anyway. So he joined her in the grass, extending his legs in front of himself and liking the coolness of the shade. It smelled nice here. The fragrance of the roses was thick in the air, and it mingled with the various other pleasant smells of the countryside.

"That's cute," he said, gesturing to her bracelet. "Make it yourself?"

She glanced at the seashell pasta fondly. "My brother."

"Ah. So, Betty Ann... you're awfully young to be hanging out at a place like this."

"You are not so much older, Mr. Herbert."

"Maybe not," Craig admitted. "I suppose you know

quite a few things about me from my profile page on the TDC website? Maybe you've checked out my links there, which connect to my other social media pages?"

Betty Ann gave him a confused smile and shook her head.

"That's fair," Craig said. "My page doesn't get a lot of hits anyway. Now, I know little about you; I hear you are a medium, right? A fortune teller of sorts?"

Betty Ann was eyeing a large yellow dandelion growing in the grass. She stroked the yellow petals gingerly with her fingertips and said, "I wouldn't know."

Craig felt a twinge of irritation. He really didn't feel like having to drag information out of a woman who knew he'd traveled so far to meet.

"Mr. Wagoner told me you knew where his wedding band was," he said. "And he told me about the warning you gave Charlie about his grandchild in Texas. Can we say this much is true – at least that you told him these things?"

"Yes. Of course, that is true."

"Alright. So, would you tell me how you've helped other people in similar ways?"

Betty Ann looked up from the dandelion now. "Mr. Herbert," she said reproachfully, "Unless it is asked of me or simply needs to be told, I don't tell it."

The statement amused Craig. "Oh, really? I was under the impression that people with your sort of talent feel an obligation to humanity to tell the world about their abilities. So the word gets out, and that way, they can help more people?"

Betty Ann shook her head. "Like I said, I don't tell things unless they are asked of me by the person or if it truly needs to be told."

"Alright. Do you think some of these people here can confirm that you have helped them out one way or the other?"

"Yes. They already said they will."

He grinned. "May I assume that you've already let them know you want to be on the Debunker's Challenge? And that you want to take your chance at being awarded the three million dollar prize?"

Betty Ann played with the dandelion again. "Mr. Wagoner told them."

"But you were the one who brought it up with him? Being a guest on the show yourself, that is?"

"Yes, Mr. Herbert. I spoke to Fred about it."

"He thinks very highly of you," Craig said. "I could tell that right off."

Craig was curious as to what fascination Betty Ann held for Fred Wagoner. Had she completely bamboozled him with her psychic claims, or was she perhaps using her physical charms to entrance the old guy? He was just about to ask her about their relationship when a pleasant-looking plump woman approached them. The woman carried a soda pop in a frosty glass bottle.

"Here you go, young man. Fred said you'd like this. Do you want something, Betty Ann?"

Betty Ann told her no thank-you. Craig accepted the beverage with earnest thanks. As the lady walked away, he took a sip. It was refreshingly cold, with tiny slivers of ice in the cola.

"Nice people here," he said to Betty Ann. "How much do you charge them for your help?"

Betty Ann laughed. "Charge them? Listen to you."

"You don't ask for any money? Now that is difficult to believe."

"They are nice people," Betty Ann said. "Well, maybe not every one of them. I don't care for Sylvia Coulter. She's a gossip and busybody. And Evan Pike can go off on his fundamentalist tirades sometimes. But for the most part, they are very nice to me. Why shouldn't I help them?"

"Fundamentalist tirades?" Craig chortled. "I thought people like you appreciate the religious hardcores."

"And maybe, Mr. Herbert, the world is just a little bigger and not as easily defined as you feel comfortable admitting."

Craig had to concede it was an intelligent observation; perhaps there was even a little truth in it. He yanked a blade of grass out of the ground and nibbled on one end.

"So you aren't asking for their money," he said. "But you want something, I am sure. Just hanging out here with old people -as nice as I'm sure they are—can't be your life's ambition."

"Could be I just dream of taking that prize money on your show?"

"That does make more sense. No one has beaten the challenge yet. But I do see the temptation in all that money. If you did somehow succeed at every test challenge you would face and win the money, you would be set for life. Not a bad payout for any psychic."

Betty Ann looked away from him again. The light tone in her voice drifted away as she said in a faraway voice, "Not bad for an Appalachian hill witch."

Craig took a large swig of the cola. "That's interesting," he remarked condescendingly. "Is that how you promote yourself?"

Betty Ann plucked the dandelion. She held the fluffy yellow head against a cheek and said, "What you really care about knowing is if I can be entertaining enough to please Gerald Agee's love of theater? He lives and breathes for the moments he exposes psychic frauds, humbug faith healers, and paranormal sham artists for what they are. But the network also expects a development of tension for the viewers. You want to know if I am able to glean enough vague information from people's body language to pique the interest of your skeptical yet hopeful audience. Can I mystify and keep them secretly yearning for proof that maybe, just maybe, there is more to our universe than what we can discern with our five mundane senses? Can I keep them entertained this way throughout the series of challenges, all the way till that delightful final moment when Agee and his panel declare I have failed and that their brilliant, scientifically designed tests have proved I am altogether a fraud? This is what you most want to really ask. This is why you are here."

Craig could not dispute the accuracy of what she said. And he did need to have some understanding of her modus operandi, so if she did appear as a guest then he and everyone else knew what to expect of her in front of the cameras.

"So far, all I know about your abilities comes from one elderly man," he said. "Tell me something about me now?"

"I know you have two assistants," she answered. "One who works on network salary, the other whom you pay out of your own bank account. You don't require two, but you felt bad for both men when you were interviewing for the position. Each was on the verge of being homeless, and they reminded you of yourself when you were their age. So you hired them both."

Craig felt a threatening touch of amazement, and then Betty Ann smiled impishly. "I'm sorry," she admitted. "Heather told that to Mr. Wagoner, and he passed it along to me. But it shows how kind a person you are."

"Ah, alright," Craig said. "How about telling me something Heather doesn't know and passed along to hell and half of Georgia?"

Betty Ann giggled. Then she fell silent and slowly began to whirl the dandelion by the stem between her fingers. She gazed at the spinning yellow petals.

At length, she said, "Kesha has always looked up to you. She feels indebted to you for paying her way through nursing school. But she wants to go back to Idaho after she gets her degree. Your father's brother and his wife still live in Spruce Grove, and she misses them."

Craig was sure now Betty Ann was a good online detective. She could have very easily gleaned this information from any social media place his sister frequented. There was no other way she could have found out such a thing.

Betty Ann continued, "You told Kesha your job pays too much for you to go back yet. That you have important contacts in California; that it is the one place you can hope to pursue the dream of starting your own film studio. But that is not really why you won't go back to Idaho with her."

Craig was intrigued now. He knew there was no other reason that kept him in L.A. But it would be fascinating to hear this mysterious reason to which she alluded.

"Okay. Why don't I want to go back to Idaho?"

The dandelion stopped whirling. As Betty Ann regarded the flower, a somber expression came to her face.

"I'll talk about that later, I promise," she said. "But you should speak with the others right now. Ask your questions. Record what they have to say."

"Very well," he answered. "But I will hold you to it, Betty Ann. I want to hear why I really don't want to go to Idaho."

Craig rose to his feet. He approached one of the tables and set the cola bottle down. The seniors gathered here greeted him with smiles and hellos. He introduced himself and told them why he was here. They nodded and explained Fred had told them to expect him to speak with them. When Craig asked if they were up to some questions and record their conversation on videotape, the seniors were happy to oblige. They even called over their friends from the other table. Every one of them was excited to share their experiences about how Betty Ann had helped them.

"Anything for little Betty Ann," one of the ladies said.

Craig took out his phone and applied the needed video recording settings. He also noticed that Betty Ann had gone back to her work on the roses. She knelt on all fours there on the grass. It was as if she didn't have a care in the world what these easily duped oldsters might tell him. It occurred to him that she, in fact, did care. He wouldn't be at all surprised if she hadn't had these people rehearse whatever b.s. stories they were about to share.

The little group didn't disappoint. Sixty-some-year-old Ann Holtzclaw asserted Betty Ann had warned her that she'd left two stove burners on at home. (At hearing this, Ms. Holtzclaw had dashed home to find her kitchen safe, although two of her best pots were supposedly stuck to the cooking eyes). Donald Wyatt, a retired policeman, related the story of the morning he'd arrived at the Center to be met by a fretting Betty Ann. She had cautioned him to get a lift home when he left because there was a problem with one of the tires on his pick-up truck.

Wyatt told Craig that by the time he left, he'd forgotten this warning. He was halfway to his home in Muddy Creek when a tie rod broke. Wyatt said the broken rod had forced the truck off the side of the road and that the vehicle did not stop rolling until it collided with a large oak stump.

Becky Fields, one of the younger seniors, informed Craig about the time she had misplaced a locket given to her by her daughter. Fields searched everywhere she could think of for the locket but without success. One day, she arrived at the Center, forlorn over what she deemed a permanent loss, when Betty Ann suggested she should ask about the locket at the Lost & Found department at the Johnson City mall. Fields took that suggestion, and sure enough, the locket had been turned over by a customer who had found it in the parking lot.

Lee Perkins, a gent well into his seventies, shared the tale of Betty Ann informing him where he would find his mama cat and her new kittens.

Eddy Bo Richards recalled when Betty Ann had apprised him that his ex-wife Diana had died (supposedly all the way down in Ormond Beach, FL). *This woman hoards everything, and she throws away nothing* Betty Ann had declared. As Eddy Bo's tale went, Betty Ann went on to inform him that his daughter would find Diana's handwritten last Will and Testament by looking in the center of a certain cabinet. This cabinet had been buried under numerous boxes of junk and old scrap metal in the hallway of Diana's condemned house. This information panned out as well, and Eddy Bo's daughter inherited the small fortune her mother had squirreled away in glass jars in the cellar of her house.

Wanda Freemont credited Betty Ann for telling her what lottery numbers to play back in March. The $46,000 winnings had helped ease the pinch Wanda faced in the ongoing effort to pay for her blood pressure and diabetes medications.

Bill Evans said Betty Ann advised him to find a new attorney, explaining that the one he'd had for years was having an affair with his much younger wife. According to Evans, this situation was proven true after he hired a private investigator.

Lastly, there was the elderly couple, Mark and April Reynolds. They were grateful to Betty Ann for advising them to install a video camera over their front porch. The couple insisted the camera proved invaluable in identifying a neighbor who had been letting her Shih Tzu poop on their immaculate lawn for over six months.

After videotaping these interviews, Craig thanked everyone who had lent their story. He walked away from the seniors, quietly amused. But he was grateful for the generous amount of contributed "eyewitness" accounts. These were old people he felt the unscrupulous Betty Ann Crawford was using. She was just the type of sham artist the TDC judges loved to challenge and the kind their drama-loving viewers tuned in to see thoroughly humiliated. Craig did feel bad for these seniors. He believed that, on some level, they merely felt sorry for Betty Ann or were just glad to have a young person take an interest in their lives. Such emotions, he assessed, were not only misguided but also wasted on a young woman who, until a few months ago, had been a complete stranger. There was always the possibility some of them just sought a little attention, and the idea of appearing in a video that might be used as part of a television episode provided that attention. But Craig also suspected some of the elderly suffered from dementia or some other mind-debilitating condition. Betty Ann had surely picked up on this and had no qualms about using their infirmities to her own advantage.

Despite the angst he felt for her artifice, he had to credit her with enterprise. Not too many mediums and clairvoyants devoted such obviously meticulous work in prepping their gullible devotees.

At the same time, it would all make for an entertaining episode. What Craig needed now was to see Betty Ann in action. He wanted to hear her tell him something about his personal life that wasn't available anywhere on social media. She would surely have to rely on a cold reading or subjective validation. All the charlatans relied on these techniques of psychological manipulation –granted, some with more melodramatic flair than others — and Craig was eager to know Betty Ann's distinctive take on it. Knowing this would help Agee in personalizing her challenges for the show.

Craig found a trash can near the back door of the patio. He deposited the now emptied cola bottle and turned to look for Betty Ann.

He spotted her standing with her back leaning against a poplar tree. She had one foot propped behind her against the trunk, and she appeared to be lost in thought as she gazed through the thickly leafy branches above. A light breeze rustled her blonde hair, and for a fleeting moment, Craig thought he saw gooseflesh ripple across her long, flawless legs.

After blinking, he saw that, no, there were no goosebumps. But they were gorgeous legs nonetheless. Craig hated that he could find this scam artist attractive. He didn't want to; in fact, he couldn't understand why he did. Most women her age that he knew either took great pains with their make-up and clothes or did their best to downplay their femininity in the effort to conform to gender-neutral fashion ideals. By contrast Betty Ann's allure was much more casual, yet demurely and distinctly feminine.

He was absently conscious of a motorized *wheeze* approaching from his right.

Wagoner's voice startled him, "I think she's got a young man already. She doesn't say much about him, but I get that feeling."

Craig saw Mr. Wagoner had parked the wheelchair right beside him. "I didn't hear your chair," he said apologetically.

"Did my friends give you enough of that information you were looking for?"

"Yes, yes, they did."

"Are you satisfied? Will you ask Betty Ann to be on your show?"

"We're getting there. I'd like to talk with her again before I sign her up. She promised to tell me about something concerning me."

A thoughtful frown pressed over Wagoner's brow. "Well, she promised to cook my supper and feed my dog. The caregiver I hired to stay with me is out of town for a couple of days – her nephew just had a baby and needs some help. And I was wanting to head for home in a few minutes. You could follow us back to the house if you'd like?"

Craig was very tempted. But he was tired, too, and needed a shower and some dinner.

"Do you know where Betty Ann will be later tonight? I can just meet her there."

Wagoner shrugged. "She plans to stay in my guest room tonight. She sometimes does when she knows the caregiver has to be away."

Craig found this piece of information telling. He was convinced Betty Ann was somehow using her feminine wiles on the old dude. But he kept this to himself.

"Okay, Mr. Wagoner, why don't I come by tonight? Heather happened to send me your address in one of her messages." Craig glanced at his wristwatch and saw it was now almost four o'clock. "Around eight? If that isn't too late?"

"I will let Betty Ann know to expect you."

Craig thanked Wagoner and told him he appreciated the help and hospitality. As he started down the walkway, he gave a last look to the poplar. Betty Ann stood there yet, regarding him with a gaze that was at once studious but unreadable. He nodded to her and began the walk back to his vehicle.

# CHAPTER TWO

On returning to his hotel room, Craig sent a message to Heather to let her know he'd arrived safely in Tennessee and had seen her uncle. Afterward, he took a shower and ordered room service. The main dish was fried chicken. At first, he was dismayed to find the meat had been cooked with the skin on. After tasting it, however, he found the flavor was marvelous. The side order of house specialty green beans was also tasty. As he enjoyed the dish, he almost felt guilty as the beans had been cooked in bacon. The sweet tea that came with the meal had noticeably been steeped longer than what he was used to on the West Coast. The beverage had also been prepared with a generous helping of pure cane sugar instead of artificial sweetener or corn syrup. Like the chicken and green beans, the flavor was authentically Southern. But he knew he'd have to keep the enjoyment of the meal to himself. One hint otherwise and his friends and co-workers would laugh and say he had gone native. Or, more likely, lecture him tediously over how much healthier their customary Californian diets were.

Craig was contemplating whether he should splurge and order a dessert when an electronic *thrum* from his laptop alerted him to an invitation to a video chat call. He sat down at the desk and moved the laptop mouse until the front page appeared. A cartoonish star pulsated over the Insti-Conference app icon. Craig tapped this, and a screen instantly unfolded across the monitor. The face of Gerald Agee looked back at him.

Agee was seated at a desk in the study of his posh home in the Pacific Palisades. His eyes were red and heavy lidded, and his expression was very relaxed. Craig guessed Agee had been hitting the weed again. The man had a prescription for it, thanks to a personal physician who prescribed it for the arthritis in his hands. Not that anyone would have guessed the wiry 70-something Agee had a single health complaint in the world. The man avoided all alcohol, tobacco, and red meat like other people avoided angry wasps.

Craig clicked the app button, which allowed audio reception and transmission. "Gerald, how's it going?"

Agee told him he had just returned from a radio interview. "It was with Zack Hamilton," Agee said. "You remember, with the Enigmatica show?"

"Oh yeah. You used to be friends, right?"

Agee laughed, coughing as he did so. "That was a long time ago. Before he turned the show into outright pablum for New Agers. But Hamilton still thinks I like him. Anyway, his smarmy listeners have recently decided to boycott our show. He asked me if I'd agree to be on to talk to call-ins. Some of those rabid nuts are eager to air their butt-hurt feelings with me. So I made Hamilton happy and came on."

Craig grinned. "I guess you gave those rabid nuts the what's for?"

Agree made a dismissive gesture. "They're a stupid lot, for sure. Logic goes over their heads. Just told them if they don't like seeing snake oil salesmen exposed then they can stick with listening to Zack's show and praying to their crystals."

"Ouch! Guess you won't be invited back any time soon?"

"Probably not." Agee shrugged. "Who really cares? I

made more money in the last six months than Zack has made in ten years."

Craig nodded amiably, but he braced for a potentially long boast session. Agee was a very successful writer, blogger, and speaker, and Craig knew the guy had every right to be proud of the niche he'd made for himself in the world of professional skeptics. Still, the man's arrogance could get out of hand, especially when he was high.

Agee scratched his balding head and licked his lips. "Anyway, I just wanted to see how your trip south of the Mason-Dixon Line is panning out so far?"

The idiom *south of the Mason-Dixon Line* was a familiar jeer, one Agee often used to describe any southern state. Craig didn't like it since he still had distant relatives living in Memphis, but he just nodded.

"I passed through parts of Tennessee when I was younger," Agee observed. "Some nice countryside, as I recall. But full of NASCAR and *wrestling* fans."

His lame attempt to mock the Southern accent was irritating. Craig tried to change the subject, "I plan to take the permission forms for the woman to sign tonight."

"What's her racket?" Agee asked. "Please tell me it's another psychic pet healer? I still get the funniest emails from the animal lovers over that last one we had on. They either adore those healers or want to see 'em crucified."

"Sorry, no. Clairvoyant. Or rather, medium."

Agee picked up a coffee cup from somewhere on his desk and took a loud swallow. "Oh well. Along with the oh, so scary channelers and basic cold read clairvoyants, they are the greediest pieces of…" Agee's next word was interrupted by a coughing fit. At last, he was able to say, "Exposing mediums for the frauds they are might be bread and butter. But boring, you know? Wish it was a pet healer, really, I do."

Craig smiled. "This one might prove more interesting

for you."

"How's that? Has this one managed to put a new gild to producing the Barnum-Forer effect?"

"I've not seen her work a crowd yet," Craig answered, "so I can't say. But from what I've observed, she is remarkably perceptive to people's emotions. She has convinced a lot of people here of her alleged powers. One of these is a well-to-do old man who has apparently opened up his home to her."

Agee gave a cynical chortle. "Not bad for an Appalachian hill witch."

The comment caught Craig off guard. But he figured the *Appalachian hill witch* epithet was just some well-known southern term, one Betty Ann and Agee had both heard.

Agee rubbed his reddened eyes and appeared to be fighting back a yawn. "Yes, go ahead and sign the gal up. I'll give her ten minutes of fame and shame. Just don't do like Heather does and book this woman at a four-star hotel. At least find a way to cut back on the accommodation perks, okay? Our delightful last guest had room service bring her steamed lobster and champagne one night."

"I've got all the paperwork ready to sign," Craig said. "I'll plan on booking her at the Relax-o-Lodge, alright? The most expensive thing on their menu is a double cheese hamburger."

"Sounds good." Agree tugged his beard. "Okay then. I'm done for the night. Going to finish a joint and head to bed. 'nite."

Before Craig could say another word, Agee closed his own app. The visuals on Craig's monitor snapped into a frame of blurry pixels.

*** 

Fred Wagoner's home was located down one of the almost hidden driveways Craig had passed earlier on Squirrel Hollow Road. The driveway was long and led through thickets to a cleared lot. Here stood a lovely old two-story house with a wrap-around porch. Not far away were a garage and a tool barn. Craig parked a polite distance behind the old car parked inside the garage. He took his briefcase from the Pacifica's front passenger seat and stepped out. As he approached the front door of the house, he heard cicadas singing loudly from the nearby trees. It was a pleasant night. The sun, which had been so hot earlier, had now slipped over the horizon, leaving a plumage of orange and purple haze painted across the sky.

Mr. Wagoner answered and invited him to come in. As Craig stepped inside and past Wagoner's wheelchair, he smelled a mouth-watering aroma.

"Betty Ann made pot roast for dinner," Wagoner said. "I'll ask her to bring you a plate if you're hungry."

"That's very kind, but I've already eaten, thank you." Craig glanced around the room. It was large, comfortably furnished, with family photographs –some new, others very old – hung on every wall. He spotted an archway that opened onto a darkened hallway.

"I am ready to talk to Betty Ann," he said, gesturing to his briefcase. "I've brought all the paperwork if she is ready to do this."

Wagoner made a little *hmm* sound as he eyed the briefcase. At last, he nodded and moved the wheelchair toward the archway.

"Mr. Herbert's here, honey!"

*Honey.* Craig lifted an amused eyebrow. *I guess because the poor old fart is drawn to her like a drone bee.*

A light in the hallway came on, and Betty Ann walked toward them. She wore a half-apron, and if it hadn't been for the girlish sandals on her feet, Craig might have thought she eluded a certain domesticity. Mr. Wagoner excused himself and moved the wheelchair to the door. Even though Craig had no doubt the man was quite capable of opening it himself,

Betty Ann hustled forward and did it for him. As Wagoner ventured out on the porch, she closed the door. She peeped out the little window there as if making sure he was alright. Craig saw an affectionate smile come to her face. But as she turned and looked at him, it faded.

Craig thought he saw perhaps a glint of reluctance in her eyes.

"You still want to do this, Betty Ann? I've talked with Gerald Agee, and if you do, he is open to having you as a guest on the show. I brought the necessary papers to sign."

The reluctant glint vanished from her eyes. "Shall we sit at the dining room table to do this?"

She led him through the hallway to a little dining room. The table here had been recently cleaned, and a hint of some kind of fruity pastry or other dessert hung in the air. They took a seat, and Craig took the necessary papers from his briefcase. First and foremost was the Agreement to Appear document, with all its many sections and sub-sections. It had been written in standard (and verbose) legalese. Basically, the document secured Betty Ann's agreement to be filmed during her appearance. She would also agree to undergo the various challenges without question, and that once all the challenges were completed, she would abide by the judges' decisions. There was a separate form that protected the network and studio from legal ramifications if Betty Ann tried to object later to this decision. Craig knew many of the show's guests refused to sign this portion, as the network wasn't overly picky about obtaining a signature on it (the consensus being that no civil trial jury would ever side with the complaint of an exposed quack).

When it came to this part, Betty Ann asked, "So I really don't have to sign this part?"

"Not really," Craig said. Despite being pretty certain she was a complete and knowing fake, he had never cared for concealing facts. "In fact, before you sign anything, I really ought to tell you that it is your right to engage legal counsel before we proceed."

She remarked softly, "You like to be upfront with people, don't you?"

The way she said it brought an unexpected flush to his cheeks. "Yes, I suppose I do."

Betty Ann read through each paper in the stacks he'd placed in front of her. When she was through reading every page, she said, "Alright. May I borrow a pen?"

"Are you satisfied with it all?"

"Yes."

He found a pen from the briefcase and helped her sort through the papers again, pointing out each line she needed to sign.

"One copy is for us, the other for you. On our copies, just be sure to add your initials –print, no cursive—beside your signature at the last line."

Except for the ticking of a clock somewhere in the house, they sat in silence while she signed. Through a small window Craig noticed that outside the sky was beginning to grow dark. He was also aware of feeling tired from the busy day. When Betty Ann was through, and she had returned his pen, Craig told her one of his assistants would confirm her plane ticket and lodgings. This assistant would also pick her up at the airport.

"Filming will begin Wednesday after next," he explained. He fished a pad from the briefcase and readied his pen. "We'll need you at the studio by nine that morning. Now, if I can get a phone number to contact you, an email as well. For any just in case scenario."

"I'm not set up for emails," she said, "and only Fred's number to be reached at."

"I can write that down. Shoot..."

"Heather has it."

"Okay," he said. "Well, I can get it from her." He was curious. "Why no email address? Don't trust the government?"

Betty Ann looked confused. "I'm not sure what you mean."

"Just a joke. But I'd suggest you go ahead and set up an email account. A social presence is important if you want to promote yourself. Of course, the network will have exclusive rights to your episode, and it will be uploaded to the show's official website. But I'm sure you might want a link for it." He suppressed a cynical chortle. "Share it; invite all your friends to view it. With any luck, your episode will be a huge hit, and you'll be famous."

If she detected his underlying enmity, she didn't show it. Instead, she thanked him for the information. He returned all the papers to the briefcase and started to wish her a functionary goodnight. Then he remembered something.

"I almost forgot," he said. "You were supposed to tell me why you think I don't want to return to Idaho?"

Betty Ann smiled. But it was a sad smile. She studied her fingernails thoughtfully, and for a moment, Craig was sure she'd changed her mind about sharing this nonexistent reason.

Her voice grew soft with emotion. At last, she uttered a single word, "Kristophe."

Craig's heart jolted. For an instant, he thought, no, surely, she wouldn't be so cruel as to show off her tricks by mentioning his little brother! He saw sorrow in her pretty face. How he resented this fake look of compassion, resented her audacity! It was all he could do to not tell her how disgusting he found her – to snatch the signed papers out of his briefcase and tear them into little shreds.

Instead, he managed to feign a disinterested tone, "What about Kristophe?"

"You still hope to see him again. After your parents died, you moved Kristophe and Kesha from Spruce Grove to California. You feel responsible for what happened to your little brother. You feel there is a better chance of finding him if you stay where you are."

Tears threatened to well in Craig's eyes. He blinked, but the anger did not subside. It had been a little over three years since Kristophe had been taken. Thirty-eight months and four days, to be precise. So painfully long since that day his housekeeper Estela had taken the seven-year-old to the park. Estela said she'd stepped away only long enough to purchase Kristophe an ice cream cone from a street vendor. When Estela came back, Kristophe was gone. No one at the park had seen what happened, and the security cameras had failed to work that day. For weeks, the police searched the area; neighbors formed a search party. Craig had put his brother's photo on every utility pole in the city. He'd paid for advertising space in newspapers with urgent requests for witness help. He'd sought assistance from the National Center for Missing and Exploited Children. The agency had offered a five-thousand-dollar reward to anyone with information about Kristophe. Gerald Agee himself had upped the reward to twenty-thousand dollars. But every lead that came in had proved utterly and painfully useless.

Over the course of the last year, Craig had made strides in putting Kristophe out of his constant waking thoughts. He told himself that his little brother had been taken away by someone desperate to have a child of their own. Someone with a loving heart, someone who would be good to Kristophe. All other possibilities were just too disturbing to contemplate any longer. So Craig had forced himself to concentrate on work and the routine aspects of everyday living. He could no longer bear to even speak his brother's name. When Kesha mentioned Kristophe, he would change the subject as quickly as possible.

In all this, Craig had trained himself not to consciously obsess on the very real possibility he would never see Kristophe again. But the truth, if he wanted to be perfectly frank with himself, was that he still grieved. He still blamed himself for not being at the park that day. And in those quiet nocturnal moments, when his mind drifted between consciousness and sleep, he still prayed for that call to come — the one from someone who would say, *your brother is alive. Kristophe is alright, and he is on his way home!*

It was emotional sadism this young woman had somehow dug up the most tragic event in his life and used it in an attempt to make him believe in her psychic powers. Somewhere in Craig's rage, his rational mind remembered that using people's pain was how these people worked. This shallow little wannabe was no different than the infamous charlatans who had come before her.

"You are well informed about my family," he sneered. "You must have spent an entire day or two searching through archived Los Angeles news stories."

Betty Ann replied in a kind voice, "You should know Kristophe is happy. But he thinks very often about you."

"What the hell are you saying?"

Betty Ann sighed. "I am telling you, Kristophe is closer than you ever imagined."

An acidy knot gripped Craig's stomach. "Shut up already," he warned lowly.

The pity on Betty Ann's face only intensified his rage. But he cleared his throat and said as stoically as possible, "And you should know you'll be exposed. You just signed the agreement allowing our panel to do it."

He reached for his briefcase and stood up. He knew he should just turn his back on her and leave. But the indignation she had kindled wasn't yet satisfied.

"I pray when you are exposed," he told her, "that old man outside will see what kind of fiend he's let stroke his delusion of youthfulness. It must satisfy you greatly to think you've got Wagoner wrapped around your pretty little finger. Have you got him to grant you access to his bank account yet? Or named you the sole inheritor of his estate? It won't be long, will it? I bet you've already taken a juicy life insurance policy out on him."

Craig immediately regretted saying what he had. Not that the insinuation was beyond the realm of possibility, but he certainly didn't want to plant any ideas in her head.

"Forget I said that," he stammered. "I don't think you would hurt him."

"Yes, you do." Betty Ann's tone was still calm, the fake compassion of her expression unflinching. "But you have no reason to think it."

The knot in Craig's stomach began to cramp. He gave her an unfeeling smile. "Of course. Goodbye, for now, Betty Ann."

As he was about to turn to go, he heard Betty Ann utter softly, "When the daisy dances with the rainbow."

He paused, feeling bile creep up his esophagus. "What?"

"When the daisy dances with the rainbow, you will learn where Kristophe is."

He recognized this as just some deliberately cryptic-sounding statement. But he was fed up with her game. Feeling bile at the back of his tongue, Craig turned on a heel and hurried out of the house.

***

Later that night, Craig took an acid reliever for the heartburn brought on by the galling conversation with Betty Ann. He had feared her bogus inferences would have him up all night thinking about his brother. But thankfully, his anger for her overwhelmed the temptation to dwell on Kristophe. He focused instead on his disgust for not just Betty Ann but every bogus clairvoyant and mentalist con like her. They were parasites, scum, every last one. After he went to bed and lay in the darkness, he imagined the discomfort she would face during the challenges. It would just be the little charlatan alone in front of cameras. She would have to face the rigorous tests to her paranormal claims without any gullible supporters there to cheer her on. There wouldn't even be an enamored old geezer close at hand to defend her from mockery.

Craig was still thinking about this the next day during the return flight to California. And by the time the pilot announced the plane was approaching LAX, Craig was able to think about Kristophe again without the memory cluttered by burning anger.

He pulled his wallet from his pants pocket and opened the little sleeve where he kept a favorite photo of Kristophe. The boy sat on a sofa, smiling as he held his newly acquired birthday present: Tomato Head. This character was one of the puppets from his favorite kids' show, Garden Adventures. During the few weeks leading up to Kristophe's birthday, Craig had been on a desperate search to find a Tomato Head plush. Local brick and mortar toy stores, as well as the most popular online stores, had all been sold out.

At last Craig came across a Tomato Head offered from a little-known British online shop. After all was said and done, the toy had cost Craig three times what he had foreseen spending. But Kristophe's joy at opening his birthday present had made the hassle and expense all worth it.

*Thank you, Craig! Tomato Head will always be my best friend after you!*

Estela had reported that Kristophe had been holding Tomato Head when she turned away to buy the ice cream.

Craig felt a tear sliding down his cheek. Brushing it away, he kissed the photo and put away his wallet.

"Are you alright, sir?"

Craig looked up to see the flight attendant. She was a middle-aged woman with screaming orange hair and a face covered thickly with frightfully pale foundation. But at his nod she gave a very becoming smile.

"Very well, sir. Fasten up now. We're about to land."

***

Kesha was waiting for Craig at the terminal. She greeted him with a huge hug and a cup of his favorite iced coffee, almond zinger. He noticed that she was wearing her waitress uniform. Her name tag was still pinned over her chest, and it appeared that it had been a while since she'd combed her sleek, bobbed hair. What troubled him was the exhaustion evident on her face. He asked if she'd taken off work to come?

"It's okay, Craig," she said. "The manager is pretty understanding."

"You shouldn't be working while you are still in school," he scolded.

They walked to an open bench and sat down. While Craig sipped on the coffee, he noticed Kesha yawn behind her palm. He offered her a drink, and she took a few large swallows.

"I mean it, Kesha," he said, "you should quit the job. I have all the bills covered."

"You have everything covered," she retorted wearily.

"What does that supposed to mean?"

"Nothing really." She gave his knee an affectionate pat. "I just don't like you feeling you have to always support me."

He gave an intentional grunt. "One day," he pointed out, "when you're a highly successful nurse practitioner, and I'm old and retired, you'll have the turn of supporting me."

Kesha rubbed her eyes. "Yeah, well, if you're living in Idaho."

"You really do plan on going back?"

She nodded. "I miss Idaho. I miss all our cousins, my old friends. Besides, they have enough nurses here in Los Angeles."

He took a deep swig of the coffee. "Alright. I don't plan on retiring from my present job title until I have my own successful television studio anyway. I suppose I can just open that studio in Nowhere, Idaho."

She snatched the cup away and drained the last of the coffee. "My big brother will make it big in *Nowhere, Idaho* or anywhere else. Just you wait and see."

He laughed, but he knew she was being serious. Kesha had always held confidence in his ambitions, even during the times when he hadn't felt it himself.

"Indeed. Now, will you give up the waitress job and just focus on your studies?"

Kesha pursed her lips and wiggled her lips thoughtfully. At last, she said, "Oh, I reckon so."

"Will you promise?"

"I promise. But I did earn enough from this job to pay for my vacation plans next week. But if you need it for bills, you tell me!"

Throwing an arm around her shoulders, Craig kissed her cheek.

***

Craig was glad to be back in their duplex, and as he readied for bed that night, very relieved to be in his own familiar room and bed. He fluffed the pillow before lying down and turned off the lamp on the nightstand. Rolling over onto one side, he folded an arm beneath the pillow. The low-key hum of the air conditioner lulled his tired mind toward sleep.

A whispery sensation touched Craig's shoulder. He was used to the air conditioner moving the sheets, so he thought nothing of this. And throwing the sheet to his waist, he drifted again toward restful bliss.

"Craig."

The small voice at his ear yanked him out of the bliss. The glow from a neighborhood light pole cast a faraway glow through the window. He saw no one in that glow. And yet the voice -one he did not recognize—had sounded so distinctly real. He closed his eyes again.

*Thump!* sounded close to the footboard.

Craig sat bolt upright. He was shocked to discover he was no longer in bed. Instead, he was standing in a grassy field in broad daylight. Trees dotted the landscape, and he was aware of a breeze blowing lightly through distant tree branches.

He heard a man's voice at his side: *"It's getting late. We'd better get there."*

Craig turned to see Fred Wagoner at his side. The old man was in his wheelchair, his legs covered with a faded, worn quilt.

Craig asked where they were going.

*"Just up that way,"* Wagoner said, gesturing straight ahead. *"You'll recognize it."*

Wagoner pressed the button that started the wheelchair motor. Craig followed just behind as the chair moved through the field. But he was confused; this place was not one he could remember having ever seen.

They did not go far before Craig saw an old, rusty barbed wire fence up ahead. The thing seemed to stretch eternally from one side of the field to the other. Wagoner stopped the wheelchair. Craig saw dark trees just over the fence. In the space between the trees, the ground was covered by a room-sized patch of what appeared to be cemented flooring.

*"You'll have to reach it,"* Wagoner told him. *"I am unable."*

Seeing the flooring gave Craig a foreboding sense of dread. He did not want to go any further.

*"I don't think I should."*

*"Of course you should,"* Wagoner said with a note of urgency. *"This is why I brought you."*

Craig took a deep breath. He approached the fence, knelt, and then lay down in the grass. Cautiously, he rolled underneath the barbed wire. Clear now, he stood up and regarded the cement flooring. He shot a look back to Wagoner. The old man was staring at the cement, his face creased with sadness.

*"What now?"* Craig asked.

At that moment, the air rang with a lilt of voices. They were the voices of children – some talking, others weeping. The sounds seemed to resonate all about Craig. He saw no one else, though, just a shudder among the tree leaves.

From behind one tree, a little boy –no older than five years of age—stepped into view. He was a white child, dressed only in faded pajamas, with a mane of glossy auburn hair. His violet eyes were deep-set and very expressive. Craig guessed the boy must be lost. Just as he was about to ask if he needed help, the boy pointed toward the flooring. His violet eyes looked forlornly at Craig.

The back of Craig's neck crawled. Something about the cement floor touched him as decidedly unwholesome. He closed his eyes and shook his head. The voices of the children stilled now and were replaced by an angry wind that whistled through the field.

From beyond the fence, Wagoner announced firmly, *"Look, son. This is why I brought you here."*

Craig reluctantly looked at the flooring. He saw something colorful sticking out of the center of the limestone cement. With slow steps, he approached the side of the flooring. He dared not step upon it –no, that was something he just couldn't bring himself to do—but he studied the thing that stuck out. Gooseflesh scoured his flesh as he recognized the pitiful thing wedged there in the unfeeling limestone. The fabric was moldy, the once brightly dyed plush now covered with lime dust. But to his heart-sinking dismay, he knew this was Kristophe's plush Tomato Head.

Tears sprang to his eyes. He looked to where the boy stood – but he had vanished.

*"I am very sorry,"* he heard Wagoner say. *"But it had to be you."*

Craig fell to his knees. The sound of his sobbing echoed in his ears. And somewhere beneath his grief, he felt a kindle of rage. To whom or what this rage was directed, he could not guess. But the grief and rage melded, and as one spinning emotional entity, lashing through his psyche.

"Craig...Craig?"

His eyes flew open. He was aware that he was sitting up in his bed. Kesha was beside him, her hand on his shoulder.

She reached for the lamp and switched it on. Craig felt the moist tears that clung to his cheeks. His heart beat with the same grief and rage he'd known in the dream.

"Oh, Kesha," he moaned miserably. "It was Tomato Head. Kristophe's Tomato Head!"

She stroked his back soothingly. "Shh," she said. "It's okay, big brother. It was only a dream."

# CHAPTER THREE

It was going on ten o'clock the following morning when Craig arrived at the studio. Thankfully, what work he had planned wouldn't take long. He had not seen Heather since getting back from Tennessee, and he was anxious to check in on her. Saturday nights were their regular buddy movie night – or, at least, until she and the father of her baby had become so close. So, he decided to get business out of the way.

Like a couple other of the network's reality series, the executive offices for *The Debunker's Challenge* were located on the ground floor of Building 3. On entering the place, he found it as quiet as most Saturdays. The only people he passed in the corridor on the way to his office were a security guard and a maintenance woman pushing a cart of cleaning supplies.

Once in the office, he dumped his knapsack on the desk. A couple of papers had been placed on the desk during his time away. He looked them over briefly, seeing they were notes from his assistant Matt. Just trivial matters: one, a quick explanation that the antique crystal Tiffany desk weight he'd ordered had suffered a delay and was not expected to arrive until the Tuesday after next. The other was about a cancellation of an upcoming meeting scheduled with the studio head of network accounting, Ross Martino. The note let him know Martino had been called out of town because his grandmother was ill. Craig was sorry for the grandmother yet quietly relieved. He hated talking with Martino. The guy came from old Hollywood money, and every meeting they'd ever had ended up in Craig spending two or more hours politely suffering Martino's boasts about his newest acquisition or girlfriend, or both.

Craig reached into the knapsack and brought out what would be needed before the filming of Betty Ann Crawford's episode. There were the papers she'd signed, which he now transferred into a large manila envelope. With a black felt pen, he marked the envelope "Legal Dept." and this he slid into the outgoing side of the tray at the corner of his desk. On Monday, one of his assistants, either Matt or Jon, would pick it up and make sure it got to the show's executive producer, Benita Shaw.

There were also some notes he'd jotted down during the plane ride home. These were personal observations about Betty Ann, or at least perceptions he'd gleaned. In these, he expressed his belief she was using a bunch of gullible old people as stepping stones to ill-gotten fame. He didn't know if Heather kept such notes when she was doing the job, but he figured that if he forgot any detail that might be useful to Agee, it was best to have written reminders.

These notes he tucked away inside the top left-hand drawer of his desk.

All that was left to do was show Agee the video interviews made at the Indian Springs Senior Citizens Center. These he had earlier transferred over from his phone to a memory card stick. He located the stick at the very bottom of the knapsack. As he looked at it, he wondered if he should go ahead and turn over the interviews to Agee? The host would get a kick out of hearing the seniors discuss Betty Ann's so-called powers. He knew Agee typically spent weekend evenings either alone at home or entertaining network bigwigs and sponsors. But he could only guess if Agee spent any weekend daytime hours at the studio.

He slid the memory stick into his shirt pocket and left the office. Agee's much more spacious office was located at the end of the corridor. As Craig approached the front door, he saw it was ajar. He knocked. A cleaning woman he recognized pulled it back and smiled.

"Marisol, hi," he said. "Is Mr. Agee in?"

"He may be back shortly," she answered. "He went to the snack room to look for spring water. But I am cleaning the windows, so knowing Mr. Agee, he'll be gone awhile. He says the smell of bleach irritates his sinuses."

Craig thanked her and headed back down the corridor. He walked all the way to the doors of the main lobby and entered. The snack room was located in an alcove past the currently vacant reception desk and directions kiosk. Craig noticed some little boys sitting on the floor in front of the kiosk who were talking among themselves. One was a plump black boy; another was a white kid with an old-fashioned mullet, while the youngest was a cute, dimple-faced Asian child. While it was common enough for the cleaning staff to occasionally bring their children to work, Craig had never seen these kids before. As he passed by, they looked up. Craig offered them a friendly wave.

Agee was seated at one of the small tables in the snack room. He was typing on the keyboard of his smartphone.

"Hey, Gerald."

Agee looked up. "Craig," he said cheerfully. "Sit down. Be right with you. I have some hilarious news, too!"

Craig took the seat across the table. A waft of heady fragrance stung the insides of his nostrils. It was one of Agee's favorite pricey colognes, something made with cedar oil, ginger root, and orris root. At least Craig thought the third ingredient was orris root. Whatever the formula was, Agee must have loved the stuff, as the pungent smell had become a running water fountain joke among the show's crew.

Agee punched a last key. "There. All sent to corporate."

Craig was momentarily distracted when the young voices over at the kiosk grew noticeably louder. He had to ignore the kids as he asked Agee about his news.

"Corporate just contacted me to let me know that the lawsuit brought by Frehley was thrown out of court yesterday."

Craig had to search his memories for a moment. "Larry Frehley? The dowsing guy?"

"Yeah, same loser. The judge didn't buy his story of defamation. In fact, she told Frehley and his lawyers that we did a public service using our detective's photos." Agee cackled. "Oh, just imagine the hell he got from his wife after she saw those? It was worth a four hundred an hour attorney's fee."

Craig didn't know what to say. Even though Frehley had failed to prove his dowsing powers for Agee and other judges on the panel, Craig wasn't comfortable at learning detectives working for the network had got photographic proof of Frehley having an affair with some gal at his local water department.

"I guess. The network footed the bill?"

The host must have sensed his skepticism, for he patted Craig's arm. "Ah, that's right; you thought Frehley was somewhat mentally challenged." Agee shrugged. "Maybe he is a half-wit, but that is no excuse for duping his neighbors out there in Ohio. Besides, I have no doubt he was smart enough to locate and memorize old groundwater maps."

"Yeah," Craig said, "guess so." The truth was, he preferred not having to think about poor Frehley.

Suddenly, he heard the sound of running feet and juvenile laughter out in the lobby. He imagined the kids were growing restless.

"I've brought the video interviews on that Crawford woman," he said. "The old folks avowing for her talents."

"Anything interesting?"

Craig gave a grim chuckle. "Their stories are sometimes quite detailed and outlandish. This woman may be young and unknown yet, but she's managed to dig her way into their hearts. I think these people would say anything she asked them to."

Agee smoothed the length of his well-groomed white beard. "Sad. But there you have it. People cashing in on the trust and stupidity of others."

"I wouldn't exactly say cashing in," Craig corrected him, "not yet anyway. But she's taking advantage of them. Especially Heather's uncle."

A satisfied smile crossed Agee's lips. "See, my boy? This is exactly why *The Debunker's Challenge* is so popular. And why I do what I do. We will expose and ruin this scuzz ball before she does any more damage."

Craig felt a heedful twinge. "We need to bear in mind she's very young, Gerald. We shouldn't endeavor to ruin her every opportunity to make a decent life for herself."

"You know what I mean," Agee said. He looked at Craig sympathetically. "But you can't feel sorry for these con artists. That's how history has seen civilizations fall since the beginning of time. When people start following charlatans like sheep they end up wolf food. That's how religions are born."

Craig hoped Agee wasn't in the mood to elaborate on this. Everyone who knew Agee was aware of his steadfast antagonism toward any and all religions. Craig admired the man on many levels: he came from a poor background yet had managed to educate himself. He was diligently health conscious, a talented writer, and he moved in highly influential circles. Agee had always maintained he'd become a professional debunker for the sake of enlightening society. Despite Agee's commendable achievements and altruistic aims, Craig couldn't help but feel he derived as much pleasure from denouncing what he termed the *gullible suckers of the world* just as much as helping open the eyes of a deluded public. And while Craig hadn't prayed or even been occupied by spiritual thoughts since he was a kid, he had never enjoyed hearing one of Agee's anti-religion tirades.

He slipped the memory stick from his pocket and handed it to Agee. "I will leave this with you, then."

"Thanks. You're as efficient as Heather, my boy. And not fat and lazy."

Craig cast him a frustrated look. "Geez, Gerald, Heather is just on maternity leave."

"Don't get bent out of shape, my boy," Agee said. "I was joking. Though, I have to say if someone is going to engage in an irresponsible social life, they shouldn't expect the network to give them time off to take care of the subsequent result. And certainly not expect the network to pay them for that time off. The farthest an employer should be willing to go is maybe paying to have the pregnancy terminated."

Craig blenched. "Well, I have things waiting for me back in the office." It was an exaggeration; all he needed was to pick up the knapsack and leave. But he'd had enough of Agee's curmudgeonly comments for one Saturday.

Agee's face lined with regret. "That was harsh. I am sorry for saying it. The truth is maybe I just came to depend on Heather, and I resent her not being around."

Craig sighed. "Yeah?"

"And I should remember the two of you are good friends," Agee said. "Tell you what; Heather probably needs a little time out of her apartment. I'm throwing a dinner party tonight for the directors of the Benevolent Hands Foundation. Why don't you and Heather come? Would love to have you."

The invitation surprised Craig. The Benevolent Hands Foundation, or BHF for short, spearheaded a lot of charity work for sick and disabled children around the globe. Agee had long been involved in promoting secular education, but Craig had no idea he was also interested in helping needy children.

"They are a charity for children. I'm sorry, Gerald. I had no idea you were a supporter."

"We all have our soft spots. A few of our network heads will be there, too. I'd like to convince them to let our future end credits feature the organization's website address or toll-free number."

Two small dark figures flitted by Craig's peripheral vision. A youthful giggle sounded from somewhere in the lobby. He wondered how long the boys would just be allowed to roam around without supervision. It was understandable that sometimes one just couldn't find a sitter, but it seemed to Craig that no one was keeping an eye whatsoever on these kids.

"What time?" he asked Agee.

"Eight o'clock."

Craig wasn't sure Heather could be ready at this short of notice, but said he was willing to try her.

"It will do her good," Agee said.

Craig promised he would ask Heather. Agee smiled broadly. As Craig walked through the lobby for the return to his office, he felt ashamed for his momentary anger with the host.

On turning down his corridor, Craig heard a pitiful high-pitched squeal echo from behind. *Those are some rowdy kids*, he thought. Curious, he stepped back into the lobby. There was no sign of the little boys anywhere, not even near the glass entrance doors or in the arches overlooking the branches of corridors. He surmised whoever had brought the children had finally arrived and left with them through another exit way.

He realized grimly this was the sensible thing for the parent or parents to do. He knew all too well it only took a moment for a child to be cruelly snatched.

Before leaving the studio, Craig messaged Heather and asked if she was up for a visit?

She answered quickly with a yes and asked if he'd be kind enough to bring a pizza over? She would pay him back, of course, but she had been craving a pepperoni and banana for days! He laughed and told her it would be his treat. Bananas on pizza seemed almost a culinary crime to Craig, but he was happy to help satisfy her craving.

After driving to Fountain Avenue, he found a parking space at her building. Craig ran to the deli across the street to order the pizza. While it was being made, he found a bottle of Heather's favorite brand of sparkling water. After the pizza was boxed and everything was paid for, he carried the items to her building. There was a steep upstairs walk to the second-story apartment. Craig was relieved when Heather answered after a single knock.

Her eyes lit on the pizza box. "Oh, bless you, bless you! I've thought about pizza all day!"

While they sat on her couch to eat, Craig thought Heather had never looked healthier. Prior to getting pregnant –and even up to just a week before—she had always struck him as a little too slender. The baby weight became her. Her fair complexion was radiant now, her shoulder-length blue-streaked auburn hair even more luxurious. She ate with obvious delight and thanked him more than once for the peach-flavored water.

"You're so good to me, Craig!"

He told her about Agee's invitation. She swallowed the bite in her mouth and gave a little snort.

"Good god!" Seeing his confusion, she explained, "Oh, I'm sure Agee's motives are pure. He may be opinionated, but I guess his heart is in the right place. Anyway, the BHF is a charity org under the direction of the Worldwide Reason Institute. You know that coalition of elite globalists that write the network a fat cheque every spring and fall? Their board members may label that money as an educational endowment, but it goes to help fund their agenda, however one spins it."

Craig had had no idea the Benevolent Hands Foundation was part of the WRI or that the network received such funding. But it sounded to him like a beneficial alliance.

"Then I suppose Gerald should have no problem getting those end credits plugged for the BHF," he said. "So, you want to go?"

Heather took a swallow of her sparkling water and said she didn't feel like it. "But please," she told him, "don't let that keep you from going."

"Nah. I'm not that interested. Just thought you might."

Heather grinned. "Hey, how is my Uncle Fred? I should have asked as soon as you came in."

Craig assured her Fred was fine. He couldn't help but pry a little, "I am curious, Heather, if you don't mind my asking…"

"What?"

"Were you aware this medium is living with your uncle?"

Heather's eyes widened. "Uncle Fred? That can't be!" She snickered. "He's like way old school proper and all that. Besides, he can't even walk. How could he possibly be…no, no way."

Craig realized he'd insinuated something not intended. "I meant he said this gal stops by his house and helps him out. And from the feeling I got, it is not infrequently."

Heather seemed more amused than stunned. "Uncle

Fred has been widowed a long time. I can't fault the man if he's lonely. Is she young…attractive?"

"Yes, on both accounts." Craig felt a shadow of the nefarious feelings toward Betty Ann that had started back in Tennessee. "My suspicion may be misplaced, but honestly, I was uneasy knowing she sometimes stays in your uncle's house."

"You mean like *Forensic Files* uneasy?"

Craig shrugged. "It's happened enough times. Some younger woman or man charms their way into an elderly person's life, just to turn around and steal them blind."

Heather frowned. "I know my cousin Michelle checks up on Uncle Fred every week. Tell you what, I'll call her tomorrow and relay your concerns."

Craig said he thought this would be wise. He also mentioned he looked forward to seeing Agee and his panel put the screws to Betty Ann Crawford.

Heather scooted to the end of the couch and eyed the rest of the pizza as if trying to decide if she wanted another slice. "She's that blazing obvious, is she?"

"Not really," Craig admitted. "She's a natural faker, I'll give her that. The world will owe Agee another big thanks. He'll have this woman exposed before she gets a chance to become the next Rosina Thompson or Miss Cleo."

Heather lifted another slice of pizza and handed it to Craig. He saw a distracted expression on her face, and a noticeably sad expression shone in her eyes.

"Heather? Is something wrong?"

She laid a palm across her pregnant belly. Tears now glinted in her eyes.

Craig set the pizza on the table and rubbed her shoulder. "Tell me, please."

She waved her hands as if commanding the tears away. But her voice was strained as she said, "I'm sorry, my mind went somewhere else. Earlier, Thad finally returned my calls."

Thad was the father of Heather's baby. Craig had not been overly impressed by the guy. He had the requisite Hollywood good looks and fair acting talents, and he talked a good talk about whatever latest cause célèbre the bigger stars supported at any given moment. But Thad spent way too much time talking about himself and whatever auditions his agent, Daniela Fogerty, had lined up next.

Craig asked what Thad had said?

"Nothing helpful," she answered. The tears spilled down her cheeks, and she accepted the paper napkin Craig offered. "He says he's still up in Canada. He's done with summer stock. Daniela Fogerty managed to get him signed on to do two commercials next month. And he's also auditioning for a movie in a week."

Craig held back his crude opinion of Thad's priorities. "When's he coming back?" he asked instead. "The baby is due in what, two weeks?"

Heather pursed her mouth angrily. "I asked, oh I asked! The a-hole never gave a straight answer, just kept talking like he didn't hear the question."

Craig wanted to kick the bum. After Heather had told Thad she was expecting, he'd acted happy enough. Later, when Craig took him out for a celebratory beer, Thad had surprised him by mentioning he was thinking of asking Heather to move in together. Then, in Heather's fifth month, Thad suddenly split for Canada. Since then, he'd managed to find time to message Heather only once. After this, he ignored her calls and messages altogether. Heather had been left in worried limbo right up till this recent phone call. Sometimes Craig wondered how Heather, as bright as she was, could have fallen for such a douche bag?

But Craig knew that had he himself spent less time

focused on work, Thad might not even be in the picture now. Over time his feelings for Heather had developed into something much stronger than mere friendship. Had he taken the initiative to tell Heather this, it may not have worked out between them. But now he was afraid he'd lost forever the chance of finding out.

"I'm sorry, Heather."

She sniffed. "I finally found someone I thought cares so much about world problems, loves the environment, respects women, the whole nine yards. And it turns out he's nothing but a self-centered jerk."

"Yes, Thad is definitely a jerk," Craig told her. "But you're going to have a beautiful baby to love, Heather. You are going to make a wonderful mom. And you got me. I'm not going anywhere. I promise, forbidding some catastrophe, I will be right there beside you in the delivery room."

Heather's face looked like it was about to crumble with emotion. "Really? You want to be there?"

Craig nodded. "You're my best friend. I sure do want to be there."

"I do not deserve a friend like you, Craig!"

"Hey, I'm being selfish, you know? I am secretly obligating you to me."

Heather made an uncertain laugh. "What do you mean?"

"It means that if the day comes when my dream comes true and I start my own film company, I will need someone I can trust to help me start it up. And the only person outside of my sister I honestly trust is you."

"You will start it. I have no doubt." She looked at him thoughtfully. "Sincerely? You'd want my help?"

"Hell yes," he said. "I've about decided to start it in Idaho. A film company wouldn't be overrun with competition there. And you know as much about the ins and outs of the business as I do. If I fail, I might as well have my best friend in Idaho to fail with me."

Hope glimmered in Heather's red-rimmed eyes. "I would love one day to get out of this place. Say goodbye to this phony, baloney town. Have the opportunity to work at a place where originality is prized, and nobody is in bed with a major sponsor."

"Then, my dear Heather, I vow I won't go unless you go with me."

She gave his shoulder a jesting smack. "Now you're going to have me crying again."

"Go ahead. Tears don't hurt. But I mean it, Heather, I won't desert you." He grinned and lightly spread his palm across her belly. He was delighted to feel a tiny limb twitch under the pads of his fingers. "Or this one."

She laughed, and the sound of it was bliss to Craig's ears. He almost felt sorry for the vain Thad. The idiot was somewhere up in Canada, missing out on something so beautiful.

***

On Monday, Kesha caught a ride to school with her friend Lucilla, so Craig drove the Mini Cooper to work. This day would see the commencement of taping for episode seven of TDC's upcoming season.

He spent a few hours in his office doing a little paperwork and then reading over and approving the last draft of the script. The contracted guest was scheduled to come in on Wednesday when the official filming would begin. This guest was one Brent Price, a high school student who lived near Red Bluff. The young man had a reputed talent for being able to predict a person's future by touching their tattoos and moles. Price's mom served as his promoter, and it was she who had first brought her son to notice by renting him booths at various outdoor psychic fairs and other such events.

Price had since then written an e-book that described how he had first come to realize he possessed a "unique gift." It had become an online bestseller. In addition to his fame as a tattoo reader, Thad and a friend hosted a popular YouTube channel dedicated to paranormal topics. In fact, it had been one of the channel's fans who had contacted Gerald Agee to boast about the teen's ability and of his achievement in the writers' world.

Agee had at once purchased and read the e-book and followed up by watching several of the kid's YouTube videos. Although Price was much younger than most guests who appeared on The Debunker's Challenge, he had an extensive fan base. And there was nothing Agee enjoyed more than taking down a celebrity hoaxer. So he had contacted Price and invited him to be a guest on the show. The boy's mother had immediately accepted on her son's behalf.

In addition to okaying the last draft, Craig gave his John Hancock for the inclusion of the two people Agee wanted as co-judges. These were familiar faces to the show: Zane Kraft, a stage illusionist who had worked the Las Vegas circuit for years, and Dr. Leslie Barkley, who held a Masters in Applied Behavior Analysis. Craig didn't particularly like Barkley; she was a woman with a caustic temperament, and who regularly blurted out rude comments to the guests. But her personality played well with Agee's low-key depreciating tone. By contrast, the attractive Kraft had an affable personality. When Kraft sat on the panel, he judged each challenge with an open mind, and he was very polite to every guest. Seven or eight times over the course of the series, Kraft had even given a number of these guests a favorable verdict. All this had endeared him to the portion of viewers who watched in hopes of seeing a guest prove their paranormal abilities. Of course, this naturally incurred for Kraft the ridicule of the cynical base audience. The contrasting admiration and loathing felt by viewers toward Kraft made for desirably high ratings. And Agee –as much as he complained about Kraft being impressionable and stupid—liked having him on for this very reason.

When Craig finally made a walk over to the studio stage, he found himself obligated to break up a heated argument between a sound tech and the delivery guy from the studio bakery. He had just opened the door to the main lobby when he heard an exchange of obscenities flying from inside. As he stepped inside, he saw a small circle of production crew standing around as the two men faced one another.

They pointed fingers at one another and cursed each other. Both challenged the other to take a swing. Craig was sure neither had the courage (or stupidity) to actually throw a punch. Still, this was not the way for any adult to behave at work. He warned that they were close to getting their butts thrown off the grounds by security. The two men backed off from each other, and Craig watched as they exited the building through different doors. Only after this did Craig learn from the other crew members that the whole thing had started over a mix-up on an order of gluten-free cookies. Craig shook his head in disbelief and returned to his office.

By three o'clock, Craig was feeling hunger pangs. He got a candy bar from the snack bar, but it didn't much help to quiet the rumbling in his stomach. At nearly four-thirty, his assistant Jon came in to tell him the production crew had invited him to meet them in a half hour for dinner over at the Ruddy Duck Cantina. Craig wasn't a big fan of the over-priced restaurant, but as hungry as he was, he'd be happy to sink his teeth into one of their infamously tasteless enchiladas.

"Why don't you come, too?" Craig suggested. "My treat."

Jon gave a shake of his head and politely declined. He said his boyfriend was planning a romantic anniversary supper at their place. After Jon stepped out, Craig picked up his briefcase and headed out of the building.

Ruddy Duck Cantina was located six blocks away from the ATN studio. It wasn't a fancy place, but the parking lot was ample. As Craig pulled in he saw a couple of his crew just entering the building. He exited the Mini Cooper and followed them inside.

The two were being escorted by a hostess. Another hostess approached Craig. She was a very lean young woman with long gold-streaked black hair caught back in a ponytail.

"Mr. Herbert?" she said, pointing at him. "I've served you and your people before. You liked our peach margaritas."

Craig read her name tag: Rose Dawn. *Ah yes,* he remembered, *you spilled clam sauce on my jacket last time.* But he only smiled sweetly as she told him his party was at a reserved table in the back. She led him to the cozy room. It appeared the rest of the party was already seated at a long rectangular table.

There was only one chair left available, and it was situated between props master David Cross and the wardrobe supervisor, Amy Pursak. Craig had no problem with David. He remembered, however, Amy was a sloppy flirt after a few drinks. As he sat down, he noticed the beer, margaritas, and wine was already flowing.

The early evening dinner turned out more pleasant than he'd expected. The food was prepared much better than usual, and unlike some company dinners, there was scant smack talk directed at any of the show's guests. This time, the conversation was relaxed and friendly. There were some jokes, none of which were very politically correct, but they were funny all the same. Amy did manage to inch her chair closer and closer to Craig's, until he felt one of her knees knock roughly into his own. She was well into her fourth or fifth glass of rosé by now. The others were laughing at some witty story Agee had just told. Amy laced her long, manicured fingers across Craig's forearm. Her big hazel eyes were a little glassy above her pretty feline smile. Craig had often thought it was a shame the only time Amy was able to conjure up a conversation without vulgarity-peppered sentences was when she was drunk.

"So how are you, Craig?" she asked thickly.

"Doing great, Amy. Yourself?"

As luck would have it, her answer was interrupted when a couple of the other women excused themselves to go to the restroom. Amy blew him a kiss and decided to go with them. Craig used the opportunity to give his goodnights and pay his share of the bill.

As Craig exited the restaurant, the last glorious rays of daylight stretched across the sky. He was good and full and looked forward to going home and watching the evening news. He would call Heather, too, if just to see how she was feeling.

He was nearly to the Mini Cooper when he spotted a child standing at the driver's door. The child was quite young, maybe three or four, with very short dark hair. He clutched what appeared to be a dark scarf to one cheek. Craig came toward him, looking here and there across the parking lot for a sign of the kid's parents. But he saw no one except a few people entering the restaurant.

"Hey buddy," he said to the boy. "Are you lost?"

The boy cast him an uncertain look. Craig saw clearly now that the thing he'd thought was a scarf was actually an old baby blanket. The boy pointed in the direction of the restaurant with a plump forefinger. A disquieted frown crimped his brow.

Craig was worried for the kid and wondered if he should take him inside the restaurant to look for his mom and dad. He bent forward, hands on his thighs.

"Is your Mommy inside the building?" he asked.

The boy answered with an indiscernible grunt.

Craig patted his little shoulder. "Don't worry, buddy. We'll go look for her."

He reached for the child's hand. This was when he heard his name spoken. He saw it was Agee, standing just behind the next car.

Agee frowned. "Were you talking to someone?"

"Yeah, this little guy." Craig gestured to the kid and saw he had slipped away. He felt a note of panic to think the young child could be running around the parking lot. Quickly, he gave a look over the place. He saw no trace of the boy. He walked away from his vehicle to the middle of the lot for a better look between the parked vehicles. But again, he found no sign of the boy.

"Did you see him?" he asked Agee.

Agee shook his head. "No. Just you."

Craig knew he was probably overreacting, but he could not just dismiss the kid.

"I meant to return this to you inside," Agee said. He took from his shirt pocket the memory stick Craig had given him on Saturday.

Agee snickered as he returned it to Craig. "Those interviews are something else. I got the feeling Ms. Crawford has promised these old fools some of the prize money she intends to win. Just can't imagine any unknown medium finding that many gullible suckers -with that many creative stories — in one old folks home."

Craig was still concerned about the boy. "Not an old folks home. A seniors center," he corrected Agee in a distracted voice. He heard himself repeat Fred Wagoner's description, "More like a club."

"Oh." Agee nodded. "Whatever it is, I will devise some very telling challenges for their Betty Ann. She'll be so painfully exposed they won't want her back in *Whereverville, Tennessee.*"

"Squirrel Hollow," Craig said, stuffing the memory stick into his pants pocket. "In the Indian Springs community."

He barely saw the curious pucker Agee gave him. "I'll see you tomorrow then, Craig? I'm going back inside."

Craig said goodnight but hardly noticed as the host made his way back inside the restaurant. He walked through the parking lot instead, searching for the boy between the vehicles and the cement pathway that led around the building. Having no luck, he got down on hands and knees beside each vehicle and looked underneath them. At length, he decided it was useless. He'd have better luck, if any, inside the Ruddy Duck.

As he started to head back inside when a new vehicle entered the parking lot. As the driver drove slowly past in search of a space, Craig heard voices piping up from the shrub-thicketed little divide between the Ruddy Duck's property and the vape shop next door. He stepped toward the divide and heard movement under the tree limbs. The next moment, he eyed about twenty young kids walking across the almost vacant parking lot of the vape shop. They were young, every one, and though their backs were all to him, he recognized the little one cuddling the old blanket to his face.

Craig also thought he recognized among the group the same three boys he'd seen playing near the kiosk on Saturday. He squinted for a better look and, looking again, was certain it was the same kids. He knew he should go after them; ask them where their parents were? But a twinge of uncertainty resisted the conscientious voice, prompting him to follow.

He noticed one of the boys wore faded pajamas... hadn't he seen this kid somewhere, too? And the little black kid walking beside him, there was something oddly familiar about the way he moved.

"Hey there!" Craig shouted. Almost at once, he wondered if he should just mind his own business.

The group of children stopped. The little black boy, who seemed so familiar from the back, turned around. His dark eyes were bright, his smile sweet. And in his arms, he held a Tomato Head plush.

Craig's heart lurched. *"Kristophe?"* Ignoring the stone of ice in his gut, he ran toward the boys. Just as he reached them, a late model silver car peeled sharply off the highway and into the lot right in front of him. The vehicle rolled right through the group of children. A horrified scream tore through Craig's windpipe.

He was hardly aware he had fallen to his knees or that the car had come to a stop. A young couple emerged from the car and hurried to him.

"Dude, are you alright?" the young driver asked.

He and the woman helped Craig to his feet. Quickly, Craig dashed around the other side of their vehicle, the couple's worried questions babbling to his ears. To both his dismay and relief, the children were not there. He looked up and down the lot. He peered into the street. Craig realized the children were not there. And he wondered if they ever had been.

***

Craig decided to spend the next couple of days at home. He wasn't sick, though when Matt called to check on him, he said he wasn't feeling well. But the incident in the parking lot had left Craig doubting his own mental health. This concern, however, was one he didn't plan to share with Kesha.

While they took dinner at the kitchen table that night, she observed, "You're not sick, Craig. And not like you to skip work. What's going on?"

"Nothing to worry about, Kesh," he assured her. "Just don't feel myself." It was as close to the truth as he was willing to go.

Kesha made an unconvincing sound. "Alright. But if you want to talk, I'm here tonight. Lucilla and Zoe won't pick me up till seven in the morning."

He suddenly remembered the vacation Kesha and her friends had been planning for over two months ago. "Oh gosh, that's right! The three of you are going to Oregon for a week. Zoe is driving." He tried to sound light as he added, "Like California doesn't have enough beaches to visit on your break. You girls better not have plans to stow away some guys."

This made her grin. "Don't need to. Zoe says Pacifica Beach is crawling with man hotties."

He smiled, and Kesha did no more prying into why he was home. They watched some television together before she turned in for bed. Craig fell asleep on the couch. Kesha was so quiet the next morning, he only stirred when she roused him to say her friends were outside to pick her up.

"You need money?" he asked drowsily.

"Nope," Kesha said and plopped a loud kiss on his brow. "I'll call you when we get there."

Craig heard her move across the room, and then the front door closed behind her. He was asleep again in moments and stayed that way until nearly nine.

He spent most of the day listening to the drone of daytime television and catching up with bills. Kesha called him around four to let him know she and her friends had made it to Pacifica Beach without a hitch. He could tell she was having a good time, and he was glad to hear her friends laughing in the background.

In the late afternoon, he called Heather. She reported she was tired but well. Her mother and a cousin had thrown her a baby shower that afternoon. He listened as Heather told him about all the infant stuff she'd brought home. Her mood was too giddy to even think of telling her about what had happened at the Ruddy Duck.

That evening, he enjoyed a dinner of ramen noodles, followed by a run through the neighborhood. After this, he took a long hot shower. It had been a day with plenty of time to casually think about what had happened at the parking lot. He readied for bed with the satisfied conclusion his sanity was perfectly intact.

He felt the problem was merely that he'd been stressed out over little things at work and that Heather and her baby were never far from his thoughts. More pertinently, he still remembered the insinuations Betty Ann Crawford had voiced. It had been she who had made him think about Kristophe. Very rationally now Craig believed Betty Ann had used social media to delve into his past. She may have even ordered one of those paid background checks, perhaps even hired a private detective. Whatever she had resorted to get his story, she had used the info for the purpose of legitimizing her medium claims. Her callous invocation of Kristophe's name and the allusion to his disappearance had succeeded in playing with his psyche.

But it was over now, and Craig saw her for the fraud she was.

As he lay in bed and closed his eyes, he understood what he'd seen in the parking lot had been induced by the power of suggestion. If he indulged any nagging concern, it was the knowledge that only in a matter of days, he'd see Betty Ann again. He had always managed to keep his temper in control, but he had never been as angry with anyone as he was with this quack medium. The truth was he loathed her for the blatant, low-class misuse of his love for his brother.

He reminded himself that very soon, Betty Ann Crawford would meet her karma. The Debunker's Challenge would ensure that.

Craig slept better that night than he had in days.

# CHAPTER FOUR

Craig arrived early to the studio on Thursday morning. On this day, the second set of challenges for tattoo reader Brent Price was scheduled to be filmed.

Agee had previously indicated that since Price's primary claim to fame was reading tattoos, the tests he was to face should be more inventive than those typically seen by the judges and viewers. So, Agee had got together with the writers to design them. Thus, the first two challenges had been performed on the preceding Wednesday.

For the first of these, Agee had lined up over twenty people in the studio. These individuals had tattoos for Price to "read." For the second challenge, the host had obtained printed photographs of tattoos that adorned famous people. These photos were laid out across a display table, and Price had been expected to touch each and every photograph. The boy was then asked to tell the judges something about the person to whom the tattoos belonged.

Today's filming would be for the third and final challenge, as well as the judges' decision segment. This last test for Price was an ingenious one. The young man would be blindfolded and guided through a room. Here, he would place his hands –and only his hands— on the tattooed limbs of five different subjects. Price would not be allowed to speak with the subjects but expected to provide a physical description of the subject based on his psychic interpretation of their tattoo. What Price would not be told beforehand was that while the tattoos would indeed be real, none of the subjects on which they had been illustrated were living people. The tattooed "skin" was actually the outer surface of prop dummies. Each dummy was somewhat human-like in appearance, though the bodily proportions were different. The faux torsos and limbs were to be filled with a special liquid, which was circulated by electronic components. This liquid enhanced the human-like suppleness of human flesh, while the warmth created by the electronic mechanism provided a steady surface temperature of 97.8 Fahrenheit. The reasoning for this deception was simple: if Price could truly discern personal details about human beings by touching their tattoos, then rationality dictated that he'd know when a tattoo he touched did not belong to a living person.

After today's filming was finished, all the taped sessions would be turned over to the editing department. The editors generally spent the remainder of a week and most of the following in post-production. Their work entailed the trimming and collating of the filmed segments and making sure the end credits included the guest's name. The editors were also responsible for the addition of at least a few deceptive bleeps throughout the audio of the final cut. This wasn't a necessary inclusion, but a few manufactured insinuations that a guest or one of the panel judges had become angry or annoyed enough to blurt out an obscenity was a sure-fire trick for galvanizing emotions in the TV audience.

Craig didn't typically spend much time in the control room during filming. But he hadn't yet met young Price with his unique alleged powers. At nearly eleven o'clock, Craig finished up some conference calls and decided to visit the studio in the hopes of seeing the boy perform for the cameras and judges.

On arriving, he found only two people in the control room: technical director Vint Hausner and his assistant, Danny Jackson. Vint was seated at the production desk while Danny knelt on the floor beside a long side table standing against a wall of the room. Danny appeared to be rummaging through a small cardboard box there next to the table.

Craig looked at the long table. It had originally been brought in for the tech crew to keep their drinks or snacks, but over time, Vint had taken it over for keeping some personal stuff. Vint kept an ashtray on one far end (no one was supposed to smoke in the room, but the tech director was so well-liked that no one ever complained). The rest of the table was taken up by Vint's collection of bobble toys. The man had all kinds of these wobbly things. There were cheesy representations of vintage vehicles and famous structures, to those rare toys highly desirable by the serious collector of film and TV memorabilia. There were even a handful of modern bobbles powered by little solar batteries (though their wobble ability was meager since the windowless room provided little light for the batteries to soak up).

Craig got a kick out of Vint's trove. The technical director was tall, quite muscular, and sported a bushy beard. His ripped arms were covered with tattoos of skulls, serpents, and Norse tribal symbols. Not the look of a man Craig might ordinarily think of as a collector of toys.

Danny pulled something wrapped in bubble wrap out of the box. He carefully peeled the wrap away to reveal a new bobble for the collection. It was a Studebaker, of all things.

Craig watched with amusement as Danny stood up and asked Vint where he wanted it?

"Anywhere for now," Vint answered. "I'll find a permanent place later."

Vint had a dutiful eye on the taping presently coming through from inside cozy stage room B. As Craig came up beside the desk, Vint glanced up and told him that camerawoman Terri Blankenship was filming a segment bumper with Agee. The host stood in front of a blue drape background as the camera rolled. Craig couldn't tell who the director for this segment was as they stood out of shot.

"When we return," Agee spoke, "you will discover if Brent Price has convinced *The Debunkers Challenge* judges of his acclaimed ability to psychically read tattoos — and if he will go home *three million dollars richer!*"

The voice of Maisey Henderson (the show's chief director) declared from out of view, "And that's a wrap!"

The input monitor went blank, though by the main preview monitor, Craig could see Agee loosen his collar and glance at his watch. Craig heard him tell Terri that he was famished.

Craig knew segment bumpers were typically the last things to be filmed. "Did I miss out?" he asked Vint. "The last challenge and the verdict?"

"Sorry, man, yeah."

"Aw, too bad. I was looking forward to watching those."

"The judges' verdict went par for course," Vint said. "The kid failed big time during the two challenges filmed before today. However, during the one filmed this morning... well, you'll probably regret not being here to see it."

Craig asked him why this was?

A smile crept over Vint's face. "The darned kid guessed two of those fake skins for what they were. It didn't help him with the judges' verdict, but I was impressed. Wanna see?"

Danny piped up, "I want to watch again, too."

Craig took a seat at the desk, and Danny stood by his chair. Vint flipped a couple of buttons to bring up the session. Clapper images sprang up on the output monitor.

"This is single angle," Vint said. "I've got close-ups on

the judges' faces on the secondary footage."

This piece of playback footage opened in stage room C. Five chairs were lined up toward the back. In each was one of the state-of-the-art dummies. These had been positioned in a way as to resemble sitting human beings.

The far right door in the stage room opened. Agee and the other two judges –Kraft and Barkley- entered. As they stood on the sidelines, Agee's personal secretary, Katie Alberts, came in. Katie was often brought onto the show for inconsequential parts, and today, she was leading in the blindfolded Brent Price. He was a petite young man, noticeably small for his age.

"I thought he was in high school?" Craig commented.

"He is," Danny said. "But smart. Skipped two grades back in middle school."

The judges watched silently as Katie led Brent to the first chair. A blue and golden winged butterfly had been tattooed on the dummy's right shoulder. Katie informed Brent that the person in front of him was Subject 1. She guided his hands to the dummy's shoulder.

Brent's fingers roamed gingerly over the fake skin. "This is a woman," he said hesitantly, "or at least I think. Brown hair. Tanned skin. The tattoo is a rose?"

They proceeded to the second chair. The dummy here had a tattoo of an anchor on its thigh. Katie put Brent's hands on the artificial flesh there.

Brent did not speak for a few moments. At last, he said, "A man. Short, black hair. Olive complexion. He has a dragon tattooed here."

The dummy in the third chair had a black panther illustrated on a forearm. As Brent's finger pads caressed the fake skin, he shook his head and gave a little snort.

"This is not a person," he declared. "But someone has put an illustration of a wild cat here. A black one."

Craig lifted an eyebrow. "Interesting."

Katie led Brent to the fourth dummy. Its throat had been tattooed with an eyeball.

As Brent touched the inanimate flesh, he made a little confused sound. "A tall man. Balding. He has a rune tattooed here."

Now, Katie guided Brent to the fifth and last chair. This dummy had a purple and green dragon on the inside of the thigh area.

Brent's fingers glided over the tattoo. "A dragon. Green. Purple," he said. Then, with a note of exasperation, "But again, this is not a person."

From the sideline, Agee announced, "Brent, we're sure you are anxious to see how accurate you were about these subjects and their tattoos. You may remove the blindfold now."

Craig watched as the teen took off the blindfold and handed it to Katie. He saw now the teen's features were very tender, and his deep blue eyes large and deep-set. The fragile skin under his eyes was dark, and his overall skin tone had a yellowish pallor. Craig strongly suspected the boy suffered from some health issue.

As Brent looked over the row of dummies, no telling expression came to his face. He said nothing.

It was the Zane Kraft who ventured a comment, "You nailed two of them, Brent. You told us they weren't people, and you've correctly identified their tattoos."

Dr. Leslie Barkley shook her head and said in a snide tone, "Not exactly. He clearly said the third subject had a wild cat tattoo. That is *clearly* a panther. There is a distinct difference."

"I'd have to disagree," Kraft responded. "A panther is a big cat that lives in the wild. And that big cat, as we all see, is black."

Agee beamed benignly at Brent. "What do you think, Brent? Is two out of three a testament to your psychic abilities?"

Only now did Brent crack a hard smile. "I think this was meaningless," he told the host. "I have never said I can pick up information from a tattoo on a dummy."

Over the broadcast, the unseen segment director called, "Cut!" The playback was abruptly cut off.

Vint observed, "The cameraman said he was glad they cut it off at that point. Barkley replied to the kid with one of her patented *you should seek therapy* remarks. She never learns; the last time she said that to a guest, she got sued for malpractice."

Danny said, "I think they ought to test Dr. Barkley. I don't think she could have guessed any of those were dummies."

Craig pushed the chair back from the desk. "How did the kid handle losing the Verdict?"

"Like a trooper," Vint said. "He told them *thanks for having me* and wished them all a nice day."

"I wonder what kind of effect this will have on his social media following? Fans can quickly turn into haters over something like this."

"Maybe," Vint mused. "But at least he's found an unexpected fan of sorts."

"What do you mean?"

"Agee learned from Matt Price's mom that the kid's got Cystic Fibrosis. Agee was kinder during the Verdict segment than I've ever seen him. He offered to take them out shopping for clothes for the boy and to dinner before they left for Red Bluff. And I overheard Mrs. Price tell your assistant that someone here had made out a money order for her to help with her son's medical bills. A network cheque. She didn't know who authorized it, but she was in tears."

"Twenty-five hundred dollars," added Danny. "It

would have had to been authorized by one of the network executives. I imagine Agee was the one who requested it."

Craig was pleasantly surprised. "She and the boy having a rough time, are they?"

Vint nodded. "Yeah. The mom works two jobs, and the dad is dead."

"Well, the network can well afford it," Craig said. "And it is a very decent gesture. Agee continually surprises."

Vint chuckled. "Be nice if some of that decency would rub off on Dr. Barkley."

"The beeyotch could sure use it," Danny said.

"Yeah," Craig laughed. "But viewers love to hate her. And that's part of what keeps this show in the network's number one slot."

***

The remainder of the work week went smoothly for Craig. On Friday he had drinks with some of the tech crew, then home for a great night's sleep. Saturday was spent shopping for basics. That evening, he took Heather out to dinner to one of her favorite seafood places. The pregnancy appetite was working hard on her; she ate three different appetizers along with a clam plate and two pieces of cake. After he took her home, they watched a movie. Or, at least, they started to watch a movie — less than halfway through, Heather fell asleep on the couch. Craig covered her with a quilt. Before leaving, he wrote her a note saying he would check in with her the following day.

Sunday was rainy but relaxing. He caught up with some house chores and found a kickboxing event to watch. Kesha called during the broadcast. She reported that she and her girlfriends were having a wonderful time at Pacifica Beach but also that he was often in her thoughts.

After a dinner of a sandwich and soup, Craig called Heather. She sounded like she didn't feel well, and when he asked about it, she said she'd been experiencing some strong Braxton Hicks contractions.

"Are you sure that's all it is?"

"I'm positive," she assured him. "Don't worry. When I go into real labor, you'll be the first I call."

"Better be," he told her. "I'm going to be in that delivery room with you."

He heard her make a happy murmur. "Between you, my mom, the doctor, nurses, and possibly my sister, that freakin' delivery room is going to be packed. But I will be glad to have you there, Craig. More than you can know."

***

There was a steady rain outside when Craig turned in for bed. As such downpours often did, the sound lulled him quickly into sleep. His dreams were many and, for the most part, pleasant: visions of Heather holding her newborn baby… images of Kesha dancing on the beach with friends…half-memories of playing darts with some of his old high school buddies.

Then, at one point, Craig found he was walking across a great open field of thick green grass. The sky was clear, the sun above radiant. He saw a mountain in the distance ahead. It impressed him as the most peaceful mountain in the entire world. The craggy top was blanketed in snow that glistened beneath the overhead sun, and the entire ridge teemed with flowering lush trees.

He realized he was carrying a silver lunchbox. Curious about what kind of victuals were packed, he sat down in the velvety field to open it. There was a banquet of food inside: bowls of steaming spaghetti and long rolls of fresh bread, bunches of glistening grapes, and slices of fresh pineapple. There was even a ceramic flask. He opened this and sampled the liquid, finding it the most exquisite of wines. Neither dry nor sweet, it was a perfect blend of both. As he thought about which food to eat first, he was overcome with a feeling of sublime contentment.

Just as he reached for a roll, he heard something like a distant voice from the direction to his left. He looked over and saw a rickety old wooden fence. On the other side of the fence, not twenty yards away, stood a formidable-looking wall. Craig could not tell if the structure was made of stone or metal, only that he had the impression the material was something of both. He got to his feet and approached the fence. As he studied the wall, he saw the surface was marred with cavities. The opening of every cavity appeared to be strewn over by decaying vegetation and debris.

There was a twitch of movement at one of the lower cavities. This particular cavity was located no more than two feet above the ground, and unlike the others, the opening was unobstructed. Craig sensed anything could be lying in wait in that dark recess...snakes, spiders, something inhuman, or something perhaps even worse.

A desire to act overcame him. He scaled the ancient fence and jumped to the ground to the other side. As he approached the cavity, however, every instinct told him to stay back, to avoid looking inside.

He stepped closer and peered inside. Nothing but gaping, fathomless blackness. For a moment, he believed the twitch he'd seen before must have been a trick of his vision.

*There is nothing here.*

Just as the thought entered his mind, he heard distinct breathing from inside the cavity. A moment later, whoever or whatever it was let out a soft cry.

Craig shivered. He thought of turning away, but no, that would be cowardly, wrong.

*Who is in there? Are you alright?* he shouted.

Footfalls padded in the grass behind him. He heard a familiar voice: *You know this place, Craig.*

He turned to see Betty Ann Crawford standing there. She looked as he remembered her, in faded jeans and the tee shirt, the pasta shell bracelet at her wrist. A whisper of a breeze stirred her blonde locks and whipped it over her face. Craig was aware now none of this was real. It was nothing more than a dream inspired by the cruel influence of Betty Ann's real life mind games.

*You've been here before,* she said. *Remember how it truly looks.*

He covered his ears and shouted, *I won't let you into my head anymore! None of this is real!*

The vision of Betty Ann gave an accusing frown. *Remember, Craig! See it as it really is.*

He growled at the vision and shouted at himself to awaken. At once, the overhead sky darkened, and the green field shimmered like cold diamonds. A wink later, these things disappeared altogether, and he found himself standing in a room. He felt disoriented, and yet there was something familiar about this place. By the height of the room's single window, he guessed it was a basement. The walls were solid, plastered. Limestone flooring. Florescent fixture lights burning sickly overhead. A large water heater stood in one nearby corner. A vintage soda machine at one nearby wall. As Craig turned, he noticed an open riser staircase. They led up to a sturdy door of grayish green.

Craig knew this place, or at least thought he'd seen it before. And yet he could not recall where or when.

A choking sob sounded from behind the water heater.

He was too angry with Betty Ann to care who was sobbing or what anything here meant. He closed his eyes and shouted at himself again, *I am waking up now! I am waking up!*

The next instant, Craig awakened. His heart pounded, and his body was filmed with icy sweat. Gentle rain still pelted the roof over his room. The air conditioner hummed softly.

He closed his eyes and turned over. The terrifying images and sensations from the nightmare began to dim. Only a faintly glowing image of Betty Ann Crawford clung to his vision. Whether he was wide awake or asleep, he understood the devilish woman's lies had laid claim to his unconscious mind.

"I hate you, Betty Ann," he muttered.

He closed his eyes and let his hatred chase the last of the spectral image into oblivion.

# CHAPTER FIVE

On Monday, Craig discovered that nearly half the production crew was out with a summer cold that was making the rounds. His assistant Matt called in sick, though Jon was able to step up as a full-time assistant. Agee sent word via Katie Alberts that he was sick, too. This made for a slight inconvenience to the week's schedule. But the draft for Betty Ann Crawford's episode was already waiting on Craig's desk when he arrived at his office. He took a special interest in reading over the nature of the challenges that Agee had proposed for her. What he found was not unsatisfying. Dr. Leslie Barkley and Zane Kraft were again wanted as co-judges.

For once, Craig was delighted to give his approval for the inclusion of the waspish Barkley.

One of the planned challenges particularly gave him cause to smile. It required seven people to be brought in to help test Betty Ann's powers. Four of these people would be ordinary people randomly recruited off the street. The other three would be ringers of sorts – studio hands posing as people who had all lost loved ones. Betty Ann's task would be to tell each person something significant about themselves. Field production assistant Tabby Alvarez was in charge of recruiting the four ordinaries, while Agee would bring in the ringers.

At nearly four that afternoon, Craig was in his office.

He'd just finished a phone call with a local florist to confirm a bouquet of balloons and candy bars he wanted sent to Matt. There was a tap at the door. He looked up to see Jon poke his head in.

"What's up?" Craig asked, gesturing him in. "If you're sick, too, you can head on home for the day."

Jon shook his head. "I was wondering if you had heard the news about the Price kid?"

"No...?"

"His mom reported him missing on Sunday. The police in Red Bluff are still looking for him."

"Geesh," Craig said. He sympathized with how Mrs. Price was surely feeling. "I hope he's alright. But Brent's a teen. He probably got into an argument with his mom and stormed out long enough to worry her."

Again, Jon shook his head. "Not according to his mom. She told the police they were very close. She maintains nothing out of the ordinary happened before she found out he'd left the house and hadn't come back."

Craig remembered Brent Price was a very sick young man. "Well, I hope they find him soon. I know his health isn't good. How did you find out?"

"Benita Shaw got a call from the Red Bluff police department. They wanted to know if the kid had been seen around here. She's been calling all the network offices. So if we see him, we're supposed to call his mom or report it to the authorities in Red Bluff."

Craig was glad the executive producer was concerned, but he saw no reason Brent Price would come back to the studio. "I will. Though honestly, there'd be no reason for him to come all the way here, is there?"

Jon offered a shrug. "None I can think of."

Craig thought of something. "Oh, by the way," he said to Jon, "I know Matt was supposed to go to the airport tomorrow evening to pick up the Crawford woman—"

"Already on my schedule," Jon assured him. "And her room at the Relax-o-Lodge Inn is already reserved. I'll pick her up and take her there myself. Oh, and I talked to Matt during lunch and he says this cold is a mild one. He should be back to work tomorrow. Hopefully, you'll have a full team in the studio, too."

Craig forced a smile. As much as he looked forward to Betty Ann Crawford's embarrassment during the challenges, he couldn't help but feel it might be dicey for him to speak with her. He couldn't ignore his bitterness toward her, and he didn't want that bitterness tempting him to say or do something unprofessional once she got there.

"That'd be great," he told Jon. "Thanks, man."

*** 

That evening, Craig went home with a slight case of indigestion. It was no surprise, really; after Jon had told him the news about Brent Price, he'd thought of little besides the teen and his very likely worried mom.

The indigestion subsided after a dinner of salad and baked pork chop. Later, Craig took a lengthy run, followed by a cool shower. Then he called Kesha, and they talked for a while.

His sister sounded like she was having a great time. Kesha told him about a quaint little gift shop that sold the nicest locally handcrafted jewelry. She also mentioned meeting a guy, an artist, who had taken her dancing the night before. Randy was his name, she said, and he was originally from Los Angeles. Although Kesha tried to keep her voice neutral while she talked about this, Randy and Craig could tell she was smitten.

*He has pieces hanging in two galleries in the area,* she gushed in her sorry attempt not to gush. *We're going out again tomorrow.*

Craig was happy her trip was going well. By the time he said goodnight, Brent Price had ebbed away from his thoughts. He slept very well that night. In the morning, he woke up with all the clear-headedness and energy to which he was accustomed.

At the studio Matt and almost everyone who had been out sick before had returned. It was an active morning for those preparing to begin the filming of Betty Ann's episode. Craig's schedule didn't feel so burdened; he only had a little paperwork to fill out and a couple of phone calls to return.

At nearly ten o'clock, there was a knock at his door. He opened it to find Walter Pang standing there. Pang was one of the junior members of the Awareness Television Network's stable of attorneys, a slender, staid guy who looked much younger than his forty-five years. Craig had only spoken with the man a few times (most memorably at the last Christmas party). Although Pang was technically employed as a legal consultant, the CEOs frequently relied on him to deliver boardroom announcements or to seek answers from the various personnel working on their productions.

Pang apologized if he had interrupted anything.

"No, not at all," Craig said. "What can I do for you, Walter?"

Pang made a little grimace. "It concerns the guest whose episode was filmed last week. I am so sorry. It is probably really nothing."

Craig returned to his seat behind the desk and asked Pang to take the chair across from it.

"I heard about the Price boy's disappearance," Craig told him. "Has he come home?"

"I wish I could say yes," Pang replied with a ring of sadness. "One of our secretaries called the mother about an hour ago. The young man is still missing."

Craig felt seriously bad about this situation. "Do the

police have any leads?"

"The mother says no." Pang cleared his throat softly and said, "We have also learned some distressing information. It seems that the boy's video-making partner, another teenager named Aidan Joyce, took it upon himself to do something which could potentially cause the network some unwanted publicity."

"What's that?"

"A mass email to all their subscribed followers. In it, the Joyce boy apologized to their fans that it may be a while before the release of their next video. He then told all those subscribers that Brent Price was missing. But this is not all."

Craig felt a grim suspicion he could guess what Pang was getting at. "So, what else?"

"Aidan Joyce let them know Brent Price had failed on the Debunker's Challenge," Pang explained. And with a little note of sympathy, "It is possible Aidan Joyce is not aware there was a clause in the contract young Mr. Price signed with us. A clause which prohibits him from discussing the episode until it is aired."

Craig understood such clauses were customary practice; it was one of the papers he'd had Betty Ann Crawford sign.

"Well, Brent is a just kid," Craig said. He saw a cold glimmer in Pang's eyes. "What are we supposed to do now, sue the kid? He has disappeared. Apparently, he's taking the loss badly enough already."

Pang's voice was chilly, "The network feels it is in everyone's best interest that Brent Price's episode is never aired."

Craig understood completely now. The CEOs and their legal team were terrified if Brent Price had sunk into depression, the public would place blame at the network's doorstep.

"That's not up to me," he said. "You'll have to take it up with—"

"With no one else," Pang interjected. "It has already been decided."

"Okay." Craig wondered if Agee was fuming in his office at this very moment? "How did Agee take it?"

"Mr. Agee is fine with it." The touch of a plastic smile turned up the corners of Pang's mouth. "But another season's episode will have to be filmed to make up for the loss. We understand that, as the field producer, you were not expecting this. And for the inconvenience to you and your staff, we apologize."

Craig recognized the emptiness in Pang's apology. But he did appreciate being told up front if his work schedule for the season -and that of everyone who would be involved in making up for a scrubbed episode— were to be extended.

"I thank you for letting me know, Mr. Pang. This might be more of an inconvenience for the editing department than anyone else. No biggie for me, and probably not the guest scout. I'm sure she can find someone else interested in coming on the show."

Craig suddenly remembered this was not quite the truth…Heather was still on maternity leave, and he had no idea where he'd look for someone else to take the guest slot.

"Great," Pang responded. "And I hope you don't mind, but my wife is a big fan of the show. She took it upon herself to make a list of potential guests to invite."

Craig knew this wasn't the customary practice in finding guests, but he was relieved to hear it. "That may well be of help. What kind of guests are we talking about? Mediums, spoon-benders, finders of lost objects?"

"One woman who is a practicing Reiki master," Pang said. "A man who claims to be able to levitate. And I believe there is another who works as a psychic pet therapist."

Craig laughed. "Agee would like that last one."

"Very well. I have taken the liberty of leaving the list with your assistant, Matt." Pang stood up and extended his hand over the desk. "Thanks so much for your understanding, Craig."

Craig grasped his hand and shook it. He wished Pang a good day and watched as he let himself out. After the door shut, Craig was aware of a prick of irritation at his temple.

"A kid missing," he grumbled, "and all the studio heads can think about is protecting their own hides."

***

Before going home that evening, Craig headed over to Heather's place. He picked up fast food on the way — hamburgers, fries, and half a dozen packaged apple pies. Heather loved the greasy things, and he knew she'd regularly craved them over the last few months. As she let him into the apartment, she looked at the paper bag in his hand.

With a sniff, she said, "You brought me apple pies! Thank you!"

As they ate on her couch, Craig felt the tensions of the day slide from his shoulders. He was amused, though, for he could see Heather had recently gone on a cleaning binge. Not that she was messy to begin with, but today, there wasn't a mote of dust to be found, and her appliances gleamed. He could even smell the lingering fragrance of the carpet cleaner she'd used.

"This place is almost too clean to be comfortable in," he observed with a grin.

Heather was chewing, but she nodded. He noticed now how radiant she looked. *The very image of the proverbial earth mother*, he thought.

After swallowing, she told him she was glad he was there. She'd found something on the internet she wanted him to look at after they'd eaten.

"I did most of the cleaning yesterday," she said. "Today, I mainly sat in front of my laptop. I was kind of bored when I looked for what I'm going to show you. I really didn't expect to find it. But I think you'll be surprised. Pleasantly surprised."

"Yeah? I could use a pleasant surprise today."

At her inquisitive expression he explained about Brent Price missing and of the network's decision Pang had come to him about.

"Gotta protect their own butts," she quipped snidely. "I just hope the boy returns home soon. And that he's alright."

Craig nodded. "This means more work for our department, of course. Though Pang was thoughtful enough to hand me a list of potential guests. Made by his wife of all people."

Heather snorted with laughter. "*Jill Pang?* Oh, that woman has no stake in this, does she?"

Craig was confused. "What do you mean?"

"You remember Jill was a runner-up in one of those county beauty pageants, right? Well, the gal that took the title –Lily O'Keefe— is a professional psychic and house cleaner."

"House cleaner? Why would Jill Pang bring us a house cleaner?"

"Not a maid, silly!" Heather chuckled. "House cleaner, as in she cleans ghosts and ghouls and demons out of people's homes."

"Oh. So you think Jill Pang wants the pageant winner on the show out of revenge?"

"Check your list. If Lily O'Keefe isn't at the top of Jill's list, I'll be a monkey's aunty."

Craig had to admit he left the list at his office without even glancing at the names.

Heather shrugged and peeked into the paper bag sitting on the coffee table. She lifted out one of the packaged apple pies and peeled open the end. As she tugged the slim pie halfway out of the sleeve, Craig caught a strong waft of apples and cinnamon.

"Forget the network anyway," she said. "The only thing I want you to think about tonight is your future."

Craig smiled curiously. He would have asked what Heather meant, but the next moment, she'd sunk her teeth into the pie.

After eating the pie, Heather took Craig to her bedroom. She gestured for him to sit on the bed while she got her laptop from the nightstand. Settling on the mattress beside him, she balanced the computer atop her thighs.

"Ok, this place is about five miles outside of Elk City," she said excited. "Used to be timbering property until 2014, so the land isn't just virgin forest. There's a creek and warehouses –the timber guy's son had a trucking company for some time. There is one hilly ridge, though most of the property is pretty level. Twenty acres in all. Oh, and there's a small creek. With adjacent lots available."

"Slow down," he said. "Elk City? Elk City, Idaho?"

"Just outside the community," she explained, opening the laptop. "The real estate agency representing it is located in Elk City."

The monitor lit up. She passed the laptop to Craig, and he saw the page was part of a real estate website. There were several images on this particular agent listing. The first was a photo of a sprawling landscape with some industrial-like buildings. The second was a shot of a small but picturesque chalet. The third photo was a low wooded ridge. Below the images was a green arrow, which Craig assumed would open more photos if he clicked it.

He looked at her uncertainly. "Are you trying to tell me I should buy this place?"

"I looked at the full details page," she explained. "It has

more warehouses than shown here. Big, clean warehouses. They could easily be turned into studios. It's also at a price we can afford. I mean, if we both put our savings into it. And, it is in Idaho. Like you said you wanted, right? Idaho?"

"Yeah," he said. "Twenty acres, you say? Show me the price."

Heather reached over and manipulated the key, so the screen scrolled up. Right there atop the listing, Craig saw the price: One hundred and ten thousand dollars.

"Wow," he mused. "I have more than eighty thousand in savings. If I play it right at the bank, I'm sure I could get a loan for the rest."

"I have the rest of it already."

He winced. "The inheritance from your granddad? I couldn't let you do that, Heather."

A hurt furrow smudged Heather's brow. "You said you wanted me to be your partner. I thought you meant that."

"I did, honey. But I don't want to take your money."

"But I want to do this. It would be my investment, too." She laid a hand on top of her pregnant belly and gave him a stubborn look. "And also, an investment for more than just me."

Craig was impressed by her determination. "I suppose we can form a partnership. Sure…it could be our studio. Ours alone. Nobody to tell us who to hire or what kind of films or shows to make? It does sound very tempting."

"Of course it does," she said. "This is what you have always wanted. Let me at least contact the agent and speak to them? If it sounds promising, we could fly out and look at it after this season's episodes are all wrapped up?"

It was a daunting thought to move away from L.A. and take on such a venture entirely in their own hands. Yet this was indeed what Craig had always dreamed of. And Heather was obviously thrilled at the prospect. He had a sense this plan of hers had potential.

"You weren't kidding when you said you wanted out of this town, huh?"

She nodded. "I want something more than scrounging up mediums and psychics for Gerald Agee to humiliate. I want to be in business for myself." Her eyes glistened, and as she spoke again, her voice softened with emotion, "And I want to be with you, Craig. You're my best friend...and even more."

The earnest strain in her voice made Craig afraid he hadn't heard her correctly.

"I mean it," she said. "You are much more to me."

"You're more than that to me, too, Heather," he confessed. "You have been for a very long time. I just didn't think you could possibly feel the same."

Heather shook her head and laughed. It was a sweet, endearing laugh. One Craig cherished now more than ever before.

"Forgive me, Craig? It took me too long to see the shining gem right in front of me."

He set the laptop on the pillow and reached for her hand. It was small and warm and so very solid in his clasp.

"I treasure you, Heather," he said.

She lifted her lips to his. Her kiss was gentle, firm, and electric all at once. And now Craig was afraid he might start crying.

"And I treasure you, Craig," she whispered. She threw her arms around his neck and chuckled. "Even more than apple pie!"

***

Craig was in one of the best moods of his life when he arrived at the studio Wednesday morning. Jon followed him into his office with a cup of coffee and set it on his desk.

"How is Matt?" Craig asked.

"He showed up today. Says he's feeling much better."

"Good to hear."

"Wanted to let you know," Jon told him, "I picked Ms. Crawford up at the airport and drove her to the Relax-o-Lodge. And a studio attendant let me know she arrived at the proper studio door this morning at five till nine."

Craig flinched at the mention of Betty Ann. "Oh yeah, thanks. I appreciate that."

Jon puckered his lips thoughtfully. "Strange little thing, isn't she?"

Craig had to laugh a little. "I guess most of these fake psychics are."

"That's not what I meant," Jon said. "It was something in her demeanor. Not sure how exactly... but she's different."

"Dear lord, did she try to get into your head? Some of these freaks do."

Jon waved his hand dismissively. "Not at all. She seems very nice actually. Just a feeling I got off her. Oh, and her luggage."

"What about her luggage?"

"The lack of it. She had a purse, a cute denim shoulder-strap bag. Vintage, I imagine. I asked her if she had a suitcase or anything else to pick up at the airport carousel, but she said no. Honestly, I don't know how the poor dear managed to get any change of clothes in it. I take it Ms. Crawford is not the richest guest we've had on the show?"

"No," Craig admitted without any sympathy. He couldn't afford to care how poor Betty Ann actually was. When she got hard up enough, she'd go find a real job instead of leeching off old folks like Fred Wagoner. "Not until she writes a bestseller or two and opens her own psychic hotline."

"Hm," Jon answered thoughtfully. "Well, I think she's in wardrobe right now if you want to say hello."

Jon left the office. As he closed the door, Craig realized

that despite his resentment toward Betty Ann, his good mood was still intact. He smiled. Perhaps he would go see Betty Ann. Or, more precisely, watch her reactions as she underwent Agee's first challenge.

***

When Craig later entered the control room, tech supervisor Zed Ritchie was there standing near the table where Vint kept his bobble toys. Vint himself was seated at the production desk with his eyes on the monitor wall and audio board, hands ready at the switches and buttons. To Vint's right sat Danny, and to his left, audio specialist Yvette Moore. Yvette was very adept at her job and worked for a handful of television shows the network produced. She was here today for the filming of Betty Ann's episode. The work required her to keep an ear open to the live stream. If her acute ears picked up any backwash coming over the film equipment from inside the stage, she would immediately signal the director.

The filming today was taking place in stage room A (the largest of the stage rooms used for The Debunker's Challenge). Craig saw three monitors active at the production desk. These provided different angles of the live footage streaming in. A smaller screen at the upper left side of the monitor wall provided continuous general coverage from inside the stage as well, though it was only for general surveillance. It could provide audio as well, but this was presently turned off.

Vint glanced back at Craig. "You made good time. Agee just introduced the Crawford woman to everyone."

Craig stood beside Zed and saw that one of the camera monitors revealed a group of seven people seated in fold-out chairs. A second camera was aimed at the panel judges –Agee, Barkley, and Kraft– who stood watching in front of an interior wall. The third camera was directed toward Betty Ann Crawford. It panned out for a moment, revealing that she had been seated directly in front of the group in their folding chairs. Craig knew some of these people were the ringers Agee had brought in, and indeed, a couple of the faces looked familiar to him.

Craig noticed that wardrobe had fitted Betty Ann in a simple blue sundress with a delicate flower print and ivory sandals. The makeup people had not gone overboard in the way of foundation, powder, and mascara (not surprising, considering how young she was), and they'd applied a becoming light pink tint to her lips. Betty Ann's sun-streaked blonde hair had been brushed and pulled back from her face with a simple blue gingham patterned plastic headband. She looked very nice, noticeably fresher, and more innocent in appearance than any of the other female guests who had previously graced this stage.

*Visually deceptive*, Craig thought to himself.

"Which of those folks sitting down were recruited off the street, and which ones are Agee's ringers?" he asked Vint.

Vint shrugged. "Your guess is as good as ours. Nobody has told us much of anything this morning."

The second camera focused in on Agee's face as he addressed Betty Ann. "Alright, Ms. Crawford, as you've been told, these specially invited people are complete strangers to you. Are you ready to share with us what you can pick up about them?"

Craig watched screen three as Betty Ann nodded. She lowered her head a moment and blinked. Looking up again, she peered over the little group. Her face registered no anxiety, though Craig suspected her heart was pounding like a hammer.

The mic pinned on her dress caught the single perplexed sound she made. It was such a soft sound. Craig wasn't sure anyone else had heard it.

She moved forward a bit in the chair and laid her hands together in her lap. Her attention seemed focused on someone among the seven people before her.

"Grace Talento," she said.

From where he stood, Zed quipped, "A full name? I thought these mind readers pulled letters out of thin air? Letters that could start the first of anybody's name?"

In the stage room, Betty Ann continued speaking, "Grace, you had an appointment scheduled this morning with your parole officer. But he was out sick and had to reschedule. Later, you wandered up the street to an antique shop when you were approached by a young woman. Her name is Tabby Alvarez. She offered you fifty dollars to come to the studio and participate."

Camera one revealed a woman raising her hand. She was a large-set middle-aged woman with a short mop of curly dark hair.

"Me," the woman responded. "That would be me, Ms. Crawford."

Betty Ann regarded her a moment. "Cal isn't coming back, Grace. You know this. He was never good for you anyway. Listen to your children and move on with your life."

Grace slapped a hand over her mouth, her eyes large and incredulous. "Are you sure, Ms. Crawford? But Cal promised–"

Betty Ann shook her head. "You're clean, Grace. For the first time in over fifteen years. Stay that way, and stop punishing yourself over what happened years ago with Rodney. You paid for that, and now you deserve better."

Tears glistened in Grace's eyes. "Are you sure?"

"Yes, Grace, I am sure. You must accept that part of your life is over and done with. Forgive yourself as you have been forgiven by those who love you."

At the control desk, Danny piped up, "Don't these people usually just make vague references that could be interpreted as meaningful?"

Craig glanced quickly at the monitor showing the judges. Leslie Barkley rolled her eyes. Kraft had the look of someone fascinated. Agee's face was unreadable as he just stroked his beard and continued to watch Betty Ann's performance.

Betty Ann lowered her head for a moment. When she looked up again, she said, "Carlos. Carlos Argonez. You were also approached by this Tabby. She found you asleep in a tent near the studio. She had given you food several times before, on her way to and from work. This morning, she asked if you were interested in a paying job. You were grateful for the offer as you need medicine for that infection in your leg."

There was no reaction from anyone in the crowd. But Betty Ann didn't seem phased and continued, "Get to the hospital right away, Carlos. And…yes, ask to see the RN, Evana Paige. She'll make sure you get the antibiotic you need and pay for it herself. And in the future, don't go along with any plan Dewey suggests. He is bad news in the worst of ways. Being his friend can only bring you trouble."

Someone in the group nodded enthusiastically. As the cameraman focused in on this person, Craig saw it was a comely young Hispanic man around thirty years of age, dressed in filthy jeans and a tattered tee shirt.

"I will do that, Ms. Crawford," Carlos said. "Can you tell me if I will ever find steady work?"

"Perhaps you should check back with the tire store you applied with last month. They are rehiring."

"I will, Ms. Crawford," Carlos responded, his face beaming. "Thank you!"

Craig heard Vint chuckle. "Appears Ms. Crawford was on the mark a second time."

"Look at Barkley's face," Yvette remarked. "Looks like she could spit nails."

A fireball formed in the pit of Craig's stomach. He

didn't know how Betty Ann had gained personal information about these people Tabby had brought in. But somehow, she'd managed to do exactly this without Agee or his people suspecting a thing.

Betty Ann spoke out the name Amber Dirthick. She said that Amber was a secretary for a doctor's office. She even named the doctor. Then Betty Ann announced Amber had just got engaged to a guy named Lyle and that their marriage would be very happy. Lastly, Betty Ann suggested Amber to find her dog Muffin a companion. Muffin, Betty Ann claimed, was very high-strung and became very depressed while Amber was away at work.

A buxom woman of about thirty years of age lifted a hand. "I'm Amber," she said gleefully. "And Lyle and I did just get engaged! Now, should I go for another dog, or would Muffin get along with a kitten? My friend Samantha's cat has a litter."

Vint suddenly shouted, "Kitten!"

"Dog, say dog!" Zed pleaded, crossing fingers.

"No, no, Cockatiel!" Danny said.

Betty Ann gave Amber a recommendation for another dog. Zed gave the air a triumphant punch. "Yes!"

Vint shook his head at Danny. "Cockatiel? Ain't no dog gonna want to play with a cockatiel."

Craig groaned silently. He watched as Betty Ann called out a fourth name: Buddy Myers. She told Buddy that the brake pads on his car were just about to go, and he needed to have them changed immediately.

In the audience, a rotund young man with round-framed glasses shifted uneasily in his chair.

"My car is in the shop right now," he told Betty Ann. "But honestly, I've been thinking of trading it anyway."

Betty Ann gave him a kind look. "Just don't drive it again, Buddy. Call a garage to come to take it away. And

Buddy…"

"Yeah?"

"Cheryl was the one who broke into your basement."

Alarm registered in Buddy's eyes. "But the police talked to all the neighbors, Ms. Crawford! Cheryl said she was sound asleep." Buddy shook his head disbelievingly. "Besides, she passed away two months ago."

Betty Ann nodded. "She took your boxes of video games, the sound system, and your collection of action figures. She auctioned them off online but didn't have the chance to mail them. Her seller name was silverysylvia1259."

Buddy spurted, "Ar-are you sure?"

Betty Ann nodded. "I'm sorry. I know you two were neighbors since you were very young. But ask Cheryl's son Nolan about the website she used. He knows firsthand how his mother is. And he knows it wasn't the first time she sold things that didn't belong to her. One of the reasons he and she are not close."

Buddy rubbed the back of his head. "Okay, Ms. Crawford. Nolan's a nice guy. I'll do that, thanks."

Vint said, "This young lady is good. I'll give her that. None of that routine *the spirit of one of your loved ones is showing me this or that* baloney."

Craig studied screen two. He saw that Barkley's face had gone livid. An intrigued smile lit Kraft's face. And Agee stood there, the look on his face a mixture of suspicion and something close to marvel.

Betty Ann closed her eyes a moment. When she looked back over the audience, her tranquil composure gave way to something resembling irritation.

"The rest of you," she said, "would have me identify you by false identities. False families. False lives. You're just here to try and deceive me."

An awkward silence fell over the stage room, and the

four people Betty Ann had already addressed eyed the other three suspiciously.

Agee stepped a few feet forward, so the cameraman had to zero in on his face. He addressed Betty Ann in a voice of practiced reason, "But Betty Ann, you agreed to tell us about every one of these people. It doesn't matter *why* they are here. If you are unable to tell us about them, your challenge is already over."

Behind him, Kraft spoke up, "That seems hardly fair if what Ms. Crawford says is true." He gave Agee a sharp look. "And do tell us, Gerald, were the rest of these people brought in and given fictitious identities and life stories?"

Barkley said in her icy tone, "Doesn't matter if they were or not. She agreed to reveal details about each and every one."

Craig grinned. Whatever devious means Betty Ann had used to collude with the four others, she couldn't know anything about the three ringers.

But still, he did wonder who had tipped her off about them?

If Agee was agitated with her obvious contrivance, he didn't show it. He simply reiterated to Betty Ann in his patient tone, "What will it be, Betty Ann? Continue by revealing what your abilities pick up about these others or forfeit here and now?"

Betty Ann's head drooped slightly over one shoulder, and her gaze fell on someone in the group. At length, she raised an arm and pointed at a young man with a trim blonde beard and tight-fitting plaid shirt.

"Kevin Mottern," she said. "Twenty-seven years old. Recently had a surfboard accident. A tour guide for this studio. Lives with his dad and stepmom. Spent two weeks last year at the Beach House Treatment Center to get detoxed."

The young man flinched. But before he could reply,

Betty Ann directed her finger toward a matronly woman wearing a printed sundress and thick eyeglasses.

"Grayson Oliver," Betty Ann announced. "The studio's videotape librarian. Fifty-four years of age. Two children, Sean and Stephanie. Recently, she lost her mother, Phyllis. Needs to follow her doctor's orders on her diabetes diet, or she will end up back in the hospital."

The Oliver woman gasped. "Excuse me – how do you know what I eat?"

Betty Ann ignored her and turned her finger to the last ringer. It was a mild-mannered-looking guy in dark dress pants and an overly starched white shirt and blue tie. For anyone's guess, he could have been a nice little door-to-door missionary or salesman. And yet, Craig saw apprehension in his face and sweat bead over his brow. Betty Ann lowered her hand to her lap as she looked at him.

"Pete Morales," she said. "A groundskeeper here at the studio. You spent seventeen months in Mule Creek State Prison. You were found guilty of attacking your grandmother after she confronted you with pawning three of her rings and an antique necklace. You were granted early release because the parole board bought your lawyer's story that you suffer from anxiety. Anxiety, you claimed, that resulted from abuse you suffered at the hands of the very same grandmother. The unvarnished truth is she took care of you after your parents died. And she never once hurt you. But you threw her into a wall and then cracked her ribs with your own fists." Betty Ann glowered at him. "And even while the rest of your family wants nothing to do with you, Grandma still sends you money to this day, doesn't she, Mr. Morales?"

Morales' face turned crimson. He spun on his seat and threw a contemptuous look at the three judges. "You told me this wouldn't get personal!"

The voice of Maisey Henderson boomed out, "Cut!"

The filming stopped, and the three monitors turned black. But via the small screen providing surveillance coverage, the tech crew could still see what was going on inside the stage room. It showed Morales rising from his chair and advancing toward the judges.

"We have unexpected drama, folks," Vint observed. He reached over to the dial that adjusted the surveillance audio and turned it on.

Everyone in the production room now heard Morales complain to Agee, "You promised she had no idea who we really are!"

Grayson Oliver walked over to Agee and wagged a finger at him. "Mr. Agee, I don't want my personal life story told on television!"

Of the three ringers, only Kevin Mottern didn't seem angry. He leaned forward in his chair and asked Betty Ann pensively, "Ms. Crawford, can you tell me if Paula and I will get back together?"

Craig saw Betty Ann's mouth move as she answered. But her words to Kevin were drowned out by Morales' and Oliver's shouts directed at Agee. A moment later, the host threw up his hands and proclaimed in a booming voice, "I thank everyone who participated, but this segment is over! Please exit through the door to the right side of the stage."

"Oh no," Morales said hotly. "If you think I'm going to allow you to air what she said, you are sorrowfully mistaken!"

Director Maisey Henderson stepped into view. Her voice was diplomatic as she assured Morales, "Pete, your section will be edited out, I promise." And noting Grayson Oliver's glare she added, "Yours, too."

Zed poked Craig lightly with an elbow. "Appears we got our sweeps episode in this one, huh?"

While the fiasco in the stage room amused the tech crew, Craig was so angry tiny black dots swam in front of his eyes, and his stomach cramped as if he'd swallowed a ball bearing. With a hasty goodbye, he left the control room. After exiting the studio building, he stopped on the concrete walkway that bordered the parking lot. The overhead sun seemed to scorch his head, and he felt lightheaded. Without regard to who might pass by, he sat down on the pavement and drew several slow intakes of air.

The door opened behind him, and Danny and Zed appeared. Seeing Craig sitting there, they walked over.

"Craig, you okay?" Danny asked.

Craig nodded and drew a deep inhale. "I'm fine," he muttered. The feeling of wrath was beginning to pass. His vision cleared, and the knot in his stomach loosened, though he could taste bile at the back of his tongue.

He was now more certain than ever that Betty Ann Crawford was a pure scam artist. He just hoped Agee would discover whoever it was that had helped carry out the stage act he'd just watched.

"Hey, you want me to walk with you back to the office?" Zed offered.

Craig shook his head. And getting to his feet, he walked with determination back to the executive building.

# CHAPTER SIX

Craig took lunch that day alone in his office. It wasn't much of a meal, just the saltines and can of ginger ale he'd asked Jon to bring from the snack room. Slow chewing of the crackers settled his stomach. But he wondered if perhaps he was developing an ulcer? It was to be expected, he thought. His father and paternal grandmother had both developed ulcers by the time they'd hit their mid-thirties. Craig, however, would never have foreseen his career might contribute to his development of one. This was showbiz he was in, and a dream job compared to the bus driver's job his poor dad had worked at for over forty years. And yet, the antics of a single guest had made him nearly keel over in pain. He told himself he should take a break after this week's filming was over and Betty Ann Crawford was out of his life forever.

He knew the second challenge was going to be filmed this afternoon. As much as he knew the prudent, adult thing to do was to simply return to the studio with his emotions checked, the thought of seeing Betty Ann again sent a splatter of bile up his throat.

"God, I'm letting that little fake get the best of me," he scolded himself.

After finishing off the crackers, he picked up his cell phone and gave Kesha a call. She was at the beach, she told him happily, at the moment enjoying a picnic with her friends.

Craig asked if she'd seen the artist guy again? Oh yes, she answered. They were going to a movie later. How are you, big brother?

Craig wanted to lie, but he couldn't. "Was feeling a little rough earlier. Stomach acid. I probably ought to have a checkup next week."

"Oh my," Kesha said. "Are you sure it can wait?"

"Yes, yes," he assured her. "I'm not sick. Just, well, I suspect I may be developing an ulcer."

"Then you be sure to see a doctor," Kesha told him soberly. "If I have to make you an appointment when we get back, I will."

Craig felt a jab of affection. "I know you would. Okay, then. Enjoy the beach. Enjoy the movie. I will talk to you tomorrow?"

"Of course! I love you."

"I love you, too."

He ended the call and regarded the phone. He really did miss Kesha. His love for her gave him the determination not to be victimized by Betty Ann's mind games. At nearly one-thirty, he left the office again and returned to the studio.

\*\*\*

Vint was sitting alone at the production desk when Craig entered the control room. He was smoking a cigarette and, noticing Craig, made a courtesy wave through the tendrils of smoke curling into the air.

"Hey," Craig said. He noticed the desk monitors were all black. "I thought they were going to film the second challenge."

Vint got up and moved to the table where the ashtray was. "Done and done already."

Craig didn't know if he should feel relieved or angry with himself for missing it. "How'd it go?"

Vint stubbed the last of his cigarette into the ashtray.

"Somebody came away not happy," he replied with a note of sarcasm. "She may never grace our presence again."

Craig felt hope rise. "Really?"

"Yeah. You wanna see?"

At Craig's nod, Vint sat back down at the production desk, and Craig took a seat beside him. Vint readied taping footage to be run through one of the output monitors. Suddenly, it lit up, and the beginning of playback footage illuminated the screen.

Craig saw that this second challenge had been filmed in stage room C. He also noticed it had been set up similarly to when Brent Price had been brought in blindfolded to identify tattoos. Instead of five chairs, however, there stood a line of five pedestal tables. White, square boxes –all about the size of a microwave oven box– had been singularly placed open-side down over each table. Craig remembered giving the official approval for this challenge and knew Betty Ann was expected to tell the judges what item was hidden underneath each box. Craig couldn't recall what these items were to be, though, or even if Agee had been specific about them.

"I can't remember what Agee wanted put under those boxes."

"That should make it all the more enjoyable for you to watch," replied Vint.

"You're not going to tell me?" Craig said lightly. "That's mean, dude. I kind of work for this show, you know."

Vint laughed. Craig watched on the monitor as the far right door of the stage opened. The three judges entered and took their places on the sidelines. Next came Katie Alberts (today garbed in a sequined black dress and high heels, reminding Craig of a game show model). Right behind Katie was Betty Ann. She was still dressed as earlier, the image of guileless femininity. Craig had to stifle the urge to utter an obscene remark.

Agee sounded very upbeat as he said to Betty Ann, "Betty Ann, are you ready for your second challenge?"

Betty Ann glanced at the boxes and nodded.

Zane Kraft addressed her now, "Betty Ann, you see boxes upon five pedestals. An item has been placed under each box. For your challenge, you are to tell us what you believe these items are. You may begin with whichever box you like; spend as much time as you need to form an image in your mind. When you have told us what you think the item is, Katie will remove the box so we may all see. Then you will move on to another box."

At Betty Ann's nod, Barkley chimed in tartly, "Just remember, Betty Ann, you cannot touch any of the boxes. Do you understand?"

Betty Ann gave her a tight smile. "I understand very clearly, thank you."

Beside Craig, Vint folded his arms behind his neck to cradle his head. "I don't think the little gal was much appreciative of Barkley's condescending tone."

"Condescending is as nice as Barkley ever gets," Craig said.

They watched as Katie led Betty Ann to one side of the room. From here, the unseen cameraman had a good front view of both women. Katie gestured to the pedestals and said in a graceful tone, "Which one first, Betty Ann?"

Without any seeming contemplation, Betty Ann stepped to the table closest to the judges. She looked down at the box with a numb look on her face.

"Irises," she said. "Purple irises in a plastic vase with no color."

Katie stepped forward and lifted the box. The item was a clear vase filled with six purple flowers. Craig wasn't keen on the names of the flowers, but he was pretty sure they were irises.

"I'm sorry, Betty Ann," Agee declared from the sidelines. "Those are bearded irises. And they are royal blue."

Betty Ann rolled her eyes. "If you say so."

She moved to the next pedestal in the line. Katie set the box over the irises and quickly joined her.

Betty Ann looked at the box. "Slice of cherry pie on a white plate."

Katie lifted the second box, revealing a slice of cheesecake on a small white plate. The top of the cheesecake had been artfully drizzled with a reddish glaze.

"Again, sorry to have to correct you," Agee piped up. "But that is cake, Betty Ann. Cheesecake."

Kraft groaned. "Oh, c'mon, Gerald," he blurted out. "Pie. Cheesecake. No real difference."

Agee did not reply to him. Katie covered the dish, and Betty Ann moved to a third pedestal. Her eyelids fluttered a couple of times before she said aloud, "A dictionary. Brown cover."

Katie picked up the third box. Craig saw that, indeed, there was a hardcover book there. The cameraman focused on the front of the dust jacket: there was an image of a stage magician and in bold title read, "Las Vegas Illusionists: A Magical History." The author's name, "Zane Kraft," appeared at the bottom.

The cameraman got a shot of Kraft raising a disconcerted eyebrow. It was apparent he hadn't been told his book would be used as part of this challenge.

But Barkley smirked and asked Betty Ann to read the title of the book aloud.

"Mr. Kraft's book," Betty Ann responded. If she was embarrassed, it didn't show. Instead, she eyed the book curiously. At length, she opened the front cover and ran the pads of her fingers down the interior flap of the dust jacket. Unlike ordinary dust jackets, this one appeared to have been sealed or glued directly onto the front cover board.

"Ah, not quite," she said. The cameraman focused in again as, with a fingernail, Betty Ann loosened the flap away from the board. She then turned the book over and did the same with the back flap. With a small tug, she tore the dust jacket off completely and laid it to the side. The real book couldn't have been one of Kraft's. It was apparently very old; its green cover boards frayed, and the pages yellowed.

Betty Ann picked the book up and showed the front cover to the camera. The title read in faded gold lettering, "Western Scholastic Dictionary."

She turned and showed it to Barkley. "Dr. Barkley?"

The camera panned over and caught the crimson that darted into Barkley's cheeks. She looked angrier than Craig had ever seen her. But Kraft burst out laughing.

"Impressive, Betty Ann," he remarked. "Very good!"

Craig didn't want to believe what he was seeing. It made no sense whatsoever. Agee had let it be known that neither of his fellow judges would know before the challenge what items were to be placed under the boxes. Of course, Katie had known, as she'd been the one Agee trusted to oversee the props supervisor placing them there.

Betty Ann stepped to the fourth pedestal. She peered dully at the fourth box. "A coffee box. Yellow, green ribbon artwork. There are beverage bags with strings inside."

Katie lifted the box, exposing a small yellow carton. The green swirl design that decorated the sides did look like ribbon.

Agee cleared his throat. "Open it, Betty Ann."

She deftly drew back the top flap of the carton. Reaching inside the carton, she pulled out three small bags. The attached strings had little cardboard tags on the ends.

Agee made a satisfied grunt. "What do the tags say?"

Betty Ann looked at the bags. "Tea," she answered.

"It certainly isn't coffee, is it?"

Betty Ann laid the tea bags down on the pedestal top. Turning the carton over, she pointed at the bottom.

She asked the cameraman, "You have this?"

The angle focused on the cardboard and the small gold text that appeared there: Golden Mountain Coffee Co.

"Just a moment," Agee countered. "It doesn't count what the carton reads."

Kraft said brightly, "She didn't say coffee bags. She said there was *a coffee box*."

Barkley snorted audibly. "Zane, you poor gullible man! She also didn't say tea was inside of it, either. She described the content only as beverage bags."

"Okay, okay, folks," Agee said in a calming voice. "Betty Ann has one last item."

Betty Ann turned to the last pedestal. Craig noticed the anxious stitches that dimpled her brow and the hesitant glance she shot the judges. It was also apparent Katie wasn't comfortable standing close to this pedestal.

A dubious twist came to Betty Ann's lips. "You don't want this box taken up," she announced. "Believe me."

"Why do you say this, Betty Ann?" Agee asked.

She regarded him stonily. "You know."

"Oh, come on," Barkley carped. "This is why you're here, Ms. Crawford. Tell us what you believe is under the box!"

Craig noticed a slight clench of Betty Ann's jaw. She looked at Katie now and whispered something the audio didn't pick up. Whatever it was made Katie nod, and she backed up a few steps.

Betty Ann looked at the judges. "Spider. A big, hairy, ugly spider."

Silence fell over the room. Craig saw beads of perspiration break out over Katie's face.

"Katie," Agee said, "please remove the box."

Katie was frozen, her eyes wide and shining with terror.

Agee was clearly agitated as he admonished, "Katie–"

Before the sentence could be finished, Betty Ann reached for the box and snatched it up. On the pedestal stood a clear, ventilated square container, and inside of the container was a live tarantula. It moved ever so lightly, its pedipalps brushing lazily across the section of container in front of it.

Katie sucked back a gasp of air and stared at the creature. It was evident by her trembling that she was horrified. Betty Ann turned around and, seeing her distress, rubbed her arm comfortingly.

"I have to inform you, Betty Ann," Agee hailed. "That is a tarantula. Not a spider."

The camera caught Kraft face-palm himself. "Oh, for god's sake, Gerald. Tarantula. Freaking giant spider. Whatever, it's the same damned thing!"

"No, they are not!" Barkley snipped.

Betty Ann placed the white box over the tarantula's container. With it covered, Katie gave a relieved exhale.

"You should have warned your assistant," Betty Ann told Agee. "You knew how these things make her feel."

Craig noticed Vint quake with laughter.

"Pardon me," Vint said. "I know it's unkind, but my pity for Katie is lean. She keeps parking her Ferrari in my space."

It was not clear who Vint was talking about when he said, *she may never grace our presence again.* But Craig was too flummoxed to comment. Betty Ann's guesses had been stunningly accurate. He could fathom no way she could have known what Agee had placed under those boxes before she was brought into the stage room.

He heard Kraft criticize Agee, "You know, my mother

has a phobia of moths. Last time she saw one, she suffered a stroke."

"Don't be ridiculous," Barkley groaned. "Phobias very rarely cause strokes. I should know, I'm a professional doctor."

"You're not a *medical* doctor," Kraft shot back. "And hardly a professional."

Katie gave an irritated grunt and threw her hands up. Craig watched as she marched across the room and grumbled something toward Agee as she passed by. The next moment, she disappeared from view of the camera. But the audio caught the sound of the stage door open and then slam shut.

Betty Ann stared silently at the judges and shook her head.

At this point, Agee looked to where the cameraman and director stood. "Maisey, we can call this a wrap," he said.

Maisey Henderson called out, "That's a wrap!" And with that, the production desk screen went dark.

Vint moved forward in his chair and pushed the button that turned off the output monitor. "I have to say," he said, "so far, this Crawford gal is the most intriguing guest I've seen on the show. My guess is that if anyone has a chance to win the three million bucks, it's going to be her. Kind of scary for us when you think about it. If the network actually ends up having to cough up that kind of money, they could decide to cancel the show."

Craig whipped up an assuring smile. "I wouldn't sweat it, Vint. Sure, Kraft may end up convinced of Betty Ann's psychic abilities. There's even a chance she even gets Barkley to believe in them, too. But this series is Gerald's baby. It's what makes him the most celebrated skeptic on the planet. He won't let her walk off with a win. No way."

"As uncomfortably fishy as that sounds," Vint said, "I probably should hope you're right. It's not like I'm up to looking for another job anytime soon."

***

In the executive building, Craig picked up a large carton of pineapple juice in the snack room before returning to his office. He didn't speak to anyone and honestly didn't feel like seeing anyone. The fact was he hardly felt as optimistic as he'd tried to pretend with Vint. He was still trying to digest what he had seen from the playback of the second challenge. His guess was Betty Ann must have recruited some helpful flunkies throughout the studio. He couldn't help but remember the disquieting insinuations she'd made about his little brother back in Tennessee. And he was beginning to suspect that instead of wasting his energy hating her, he should pray her fraud was exposed ASAP.

A half-hour later, Craig was seated behind his desk, finishing up a call with Heather. She told him to come by after work as she was making dinner for the two of them. After the call, he chugged down the last of the juice and tossed the carton into the wastepaper basket. Just as he pushed his chair away from the desk and started to rise, a knock sounded at the door. He started to ask who it was when Agee walked in. Jon followed right on his heels.

It was apparent his assistant was embarrassed about Agee getting past him without a courtesy announcement.

"It's okay, Jon."

Jon smiled and left, closing the door behind him.

"I apologize, Craig," Agee said. "I shouldn't have just walked in."

Craig made a dismissive wave. "No problem, Gerald. Have a seat."

Agee took the chair across the desk. There was a little grimace in the host's features as he said, "Vint told me you watched Crawford's first challenge yesterday. And that you saw the second on replay."

"Yeah, I did." Craig felt a twinge of apprehension. "Our guest is something else, huh?"

Agree snorted and said something vulgar under his breath.

"Gerald, I'm sorry," Craig said. "Apparently, there's more to this woman than I guessed. If Barkley and Kraft end up believing her, it's on me."

Agee raised an eyebrow. "I don't think for a moment there is any truth to that white trash woman's claims. And I think we both know how Barkley will vote, don't we?"

Craig was a little confused. "Yeah..? I suppose so."

"I only came here to let you know that gal won't get away with it. I just got back from the legal department."

"Oh?"

"Yes. I talked with Pang, and he immediately got hold of a detective. This guy will be following Ms. Crawford's activities tonight. He and his team will find out where she spends her time between now and the taping tomorrow. Who it is she talks with, who it is she has got working for her here."

"Good," Craig said. But he had a feeling Agee was holding something back. "What is it? I can tell you have more on your mind."

Reluctance registered in Agee's voice, "Whoever has been helping her here will be terminated from their job. I just thought you should know."

Craig guessed the implication was aimed at him. "Gerald," he said tiredly, "I have nothing to hide. But your detective will be able to tell you this himself."

Agee shook his head. "You misunderstand, Craig. You are the last person I can imagine colluding with a con artist. But there are others here...and I hate saying it, but others I'm sure would be happy to help a pretty young thing get her hands on three million dollars."

Craig felt a shiver of remorse. "I wish I had never met

Betty Ann Crawford," he admitted. "I have had bad dreams ever since meeting that woman."

"For that, Craig, I am very sorry to hear. You have to remember these fake mediums and their ilk have ingenious ways of messing with people's minds."

"I know, I know." Craig exhaled wearily. He remembered something Vint had said earlier. "Gerald, let me ask you something?"

"Yes?"

"If the unlikely day was to come when one of our guests proved to possess psychic powers or healing abilities, or whatever, and they walked away with the prize money... would the show be canceled?"

"Oh, I believe it would. No network likes losing money, and ATN wouldn't take the chance on it happening twice." Agee looked at him warmly. "You're worried about everyone's jobs, aren't you?"

"Of course."

"Don't be," Agee told him brightly. "I still have some pull with the Network, even more with their prestigious benefactors."

For the first time, Craig realized how much he owed Agee. He'd only worked as a producer's assistant on two television projects before he'd applied for an apprentice position with The Debunker's Challenge. Nevertheless, Agee had seemed very impressed with his amateur college film projects and suggested him to the show's producers. After Kristophe had disappeared, it had been Agee who had fattened the reward offered for information leading to the boy's return. And despite Agee's sanguine tone now, Craig knew The Debunker's Challenge was the crown achievement of the man's life work. Craig hated the prospect of the guy losing his show. It struck Craig as especially wrong if such a loss were to happen because of misdeeds perpetuated by the very kind of swindler Agee had dedicated his life to exposing.

Craig felt a fond lump in his throat. "Gerald," he asked, "why do you do what you do? Discredit all these useless people, that is?"

"You wound me," Agee said with a jovial air. "Haven't you already read all the embarrassingly self-promotional bio stuff on my blog?"

"I've read your biography, of course. All that stuff about when you were a kid who loved to solve mysteries nobody else could crack. Your years spent learning how stage illusionists pull off their tricks. And how later you learned to see through the tricks of even the most experienced shyster."

"Well," Agee replied, smiling. "I was too lazy to go into law enforcement and become a proper detective."

Craig drew a thoughtful breath. "But you've never detoured from your one objective. It's been your life's work. I can't help but think such motivation is rooted out of something more than showing the world how Blackstone pulled rabbits out of a hat. Am I right?"

Agee stroked his beard. "To be candid, you're right. Not that it's anything I want to bore my followers and fans with. It's not something I even think about much anymore. I doubt it'll ever appear in a book of memoirs. But yes. There was another motivation. In the beginning, anyway."

"I'd love to know what it was," Craig told him. "I promise it won't go further than this room."

"Perhaps I should tell you," Agee said. "It might help you understand why I advise so strongly against letting shysters work on your mind. The truth is, my friend, it was my mother who originally inspired my interest in debunking the frauds of this world."

Craig was surprised. "Yeah? Your mom enjoyed solving mysteries, too?"

Agee's eyes squinted, and the corners of his mouth

turned up stiffly. "No. Mother liked believing in mysteries." Seeing the confusion in Craig's face, he elaborated, "Mother was a very spiritual woman, you see. She was born in Ireland. Her family were all gypsies, or for your politically correct ears, *Irish Travelers*. As superstitious people as they come. Tarot readers, storm seers, star diviners, omen watchers, and such. It was rather alarming as a kid to hear my mother mark down every change in the weather or run-of-the-mill mishap to some augury or sign or curse. And I grew up wanting to challenge her superstitions.

"Now, Mother also had this one cousin, Madge, who made a living as a so-called mind reader. One day, I showed Mother how Madge did it. It was all a matter of studying people's reactions and giving them leading questions. After this, I started taking Mother to magic shows. She always had an unhealthy affection for those things. I would explain to her how the tricks she saw on stage were performed. I don't think she was very keen about having her illusions broken, but she'd go. I think just in the hopes that I was proven wrong.

"Then, when I was a teenager, I asked her to come with me to a tent show where a traveling minister had been performing for several days. You know the kind; those who claim they can make the paralyzed walk and cure the sick of cancer and such things. Mother had her own religious beliefs and wasn't an evangelical like this guy described himself, but she agreed to go. When we got there, I told Mother to go ahead and take a seat inside. Meanwhile, I walked around to the back of the tent. The day earlier, I had hidden a pair of crutches in the bushes there. I'd borrowed the crutches from my neighbor Luke, who had broken a leg earlier that year. Anyway, I came back into the tent, walking with the crutches. I must have put on a good performance, as his audience had no idea I wasn't really crippled. Their dear preacher had already started his act, and he conveniently almost skipped over me. Then, a couple of people in the crowd noticed and shouted out, *here's another one!* So the quack had little choice but to call me forward. He pressed his Bible over my brow and started blabbering in his tongues bit. This went on for a few minutes when, finally, he yelled *You are healed, little brother!* I just looked at the man with a big, hopeful grin on my face. I threw those crutches down and took a step. His crowd began to cheer and clap and praise their god. This was until I fell to my knees, screaming. I cried and blubbered and told the preacher he hadn't cured a thing! Oh, you should have seen the look on the faces of his audience! The preacher tried to save face, of course, and told me to come back that evening for a personal *laying on of hands.* I retrieved the crutches and limped out of there. And let me tell you, as I walked through the sweaty throng, I saw more than a few doubtful glares aimed at that humiliated preacher.

"But my poor horrified Mother, she was anything but impressed by my performance. When we got home later, she told me I was possessed by the evil one himself. She was going to call in her Uncle Max and have him exorcize the demon or demons! It was then and there that I decided I'd had enough. I stuffed some of my things into a duffle bag and left. That night, I found a job as a roadie with a second-rate rock band that was passing through town. I left with them. Eventually, they stopped in Las Vegas, and I found a better paying gig as a stage mentalist's assistant. Cayo Fitzsimmons, that was his name. He played in small theaters and venues throughout the fifty states. He never got rich from it, but he was doing what he felt called to do. Fitzsimmons was the first to teach me how to prompt people to believe I knew all about them…by reading expressions on their faces. The way someone's mouth moves when they smile or frown. Their posture. The way their hands move. How often they blink. The subtle differences in tone of speech. Fitzsimmons also taught me the vital art of recognizing when someone else is trying to dupe me. And the rest, as they say, is history."

Agee made a derisive scoff. "Not that even an experienced mentalist always uses common sense. That's how Fitzsimmons ended up getting himself duped by falling head over heels for some tarot reader-slash-holistic healer. A real piece of work, that one. I tried to warn him about her, but did he listen? She made him doubt his life's work, and he got interested in her metaphysical mumbo jumbo. To make a long story short, he allowed her to come between us. I finally got fed up with it and left. Last I heard, Fitzsimmons eventually moved to upstate New York, where he opened an esoteric bookstore and later died a near pauper. But I was fine. I was still determined. I vowed never to allow myself to be hoodwinked by superstition like my ignorant mother; I remembered the lessons learned from Fitzsimmons before he took the plunge into loony lake. And I can proudly say I have kept that vow to this day."

Craig shook his head sympathetically. "Pathetic. And I can understand why you've never written about or mentioned your mom to the public. It's commendable. But did her opinion of you change once you become a celebrity?"

"Oh no," Agee answered with a faded smile. "The last time we spoke, she begged me to *open my heart and see what the eyes cannot.* As if the poor old thing ever had a clue as to what was real and what wasn't."

Craig thought about Betty Ann again. He was still uneasy about what she had managed to do so far in front of the camera. How long, he wondered, would her tricks continue to torment him? He knew that the first step to ending her hold over his subconscious mind lay in somehow dismissing her from his conscious thoughts.

"Tell me, Gerald," he asked, "how do you forget them? These charlatans and quacks? How do you cleanse your brain of the mind-foolery they've ridden your waking and dreaming thoughts with?"

"Ah, that part is simple," Agee said. "When your thoughts stray to someone you don't need to think about, instead of seeing them, imagine their features turning to nothing more than smoke. Billowy smoke that you can blow away with only the will of your mind's eye. Practice doing this enough and it becomes quite easy. An associate who once worked as a criminal psychologist taught me this trick. It works, Craig, believe me. Train yourself to see people as mere smoke, and in time, you can forget anyone's face."

"Really? That nearly sounds too easy."

"Let's put it this way," Agee replied, "if asked, I couldn't describe to you my mother's face."

Craig thought this was one of the saddest things he'd ever heard. But he knew it was intrusive to ask Agee why he had chosen to forget what his mother looked like.

"Thank you for the suggestion. I will be sure to try it."

Agee rose from the chair. "Good to hear. You'll be a much happier camper."

"I hope the detective is successful. Keep me posted?"

Agee nodded. "I will, just as soon as I hear anything." He took a step toward the door and then paused. Looking at Craig, he asked, "Will you be watching the live taping of Crawford's last challenge?"

Craig felt much less stressed over Betty Ann now. "You couldn't keep me away, Gerald."

# CHAPTER SEVEN

At Heather's place, Craig was ushered to the little table in her kitchen. There, she feasted him with pasta salad and grilled Tilapia. There was even homemade mint chocolate pie for dessert. Craig was surprised Heather had prepared everything herself and delighted by how tasty the food was.

"Being stuck at home has improved your cooking skills," he teased.

"Have to fill the hours somehow," she said. "Though I confess that I'll never make a mint chocolate pie as well as my grandma."

"It's probably rare anyone cooks as well as their grandma."

She nodded and suddenly broke into a yawn behind her hands. Craig saw now how very tired she looked.

"Why don't you prop yourself up on the couch while I take care of the dishes?"

Heather accepted the suggestion. "My eyes could use a little rest."

As Heather got up from the table, Craig noticed how huge her belly had become. There was a very decided waddle to her steps, too. And if his calculations were correct, she was very near her thirty-eighth week of pregnancy.

*She might well go into labor any time now,* he thought.

After she left the room, Craig washed the dishes they'd

used, as well as the pots and pans Heather had used to make dinner. He gave the counters and table a good wipe-down. When he was finished, he walked into the living room. Heather was laid across the couch with her eyes closed. She was not quite snoring, but her breathing was deep and regular, so that he knew she was asleep.

Craig took the opportunity to hook her phone into the recharger kept on an antique table in the hallway near her bedroom door. He locked the back door, which opened to the fire escape, and turned her television to a music channel she was fond of. He set the volume low and then went to find a blanket from the bedroom closet. This he carried out to the living room and spread it across her.

Crouching beside her, he stroked her hair. "Heather? Heather, I'm going now."

Her eyelids fluttered open. Her lips turned up in a groggy smile. "Okay, Craig."

"You call me if you need anything, alright?"

"Yes," she answered softly. Her eyes closed, and the deep breathing commenced again.

Craig kissed her cheek. As he left, he locked the front door with the extra key she'd given him the year before.

***

Nightfall had just settled in when Craig pulled into his driveway. It was a muggy night, and once inside the duplex, he turned the air conditioning up and pulled off his shirt. He wanted to be in bed early so he could wake up fresh for the filming of Betty Ann's last challenge.

Unfortunately, he wasn't particularly tired, and once in bed, he found himself re-seeing what had appeared to be Betty Ann's seeming triumphs during the first two challenges. He wondered what she was doing at the moment – sitting in her motel room, laughing at Agee, laughing at all of them? And what was Pang's detective discovering at this very moment?

He also thought about Heather. On the drive home, he'd noticed the rising moon. It was big and buttery yellow that night, and he well recalled his mother saying that most babies arrived with the full moon. If that wasn't an entirely full moon he'd observed, he knew one couldn't be far off.

Craig got up and walked to the kitchen. He took a bottle of beer out of the refrigerator and carried it out to the front porch. Without a light on out here, he was able to see stars glinting in the velvety sky. He looked for the moon before remembering it would be a while before it was visible from this Western view. So he sat down at the top of the porch steps and opened the beer.

The traffic outside was rather light, and the whole neighborhood seemed particularly peaceful. Of course, most of his neighbors were youngish, with children that went to bed fairly early. The couple who occupied the other side of the duplex –Jason and Lynette– must have been out, as their vehicle was absent from their driveway. Craig heard crickets chirping loudly from the trees and grass. From somewhere not far away, music strummed out of somebody's open window. He looked across the street and admired the scenery of the Hollywood Hills, which stretched across the low horizon. The hills were only a few miles away, so Craig was able to make out the house lights that twinkled among the dark, sleepy foliage. Every little bit, he saw a flash of headlights as an occasional car winded down Queens Road.

A refrain of faraway voices erupted from the north end of the neighborhood. A moment later, Craig heard the sound of running feet –what seemed more like *multiple* feet– approaching along the sidewalk from that direction. Illumination from the streetlights gave no indication of anyone coming, and yet the pounding footfalls grew more pronounced. Curious, he set the beer down and got up. Walking down the steps, he stood on the narrow flagstone path leading to the sidewalk. He looked down the sidewalk and across the street but saw no one. The voices quieted, even as the sound of runners continued to advance.

Suddenly, he heard the mass of feet sprint across the sidewalk in front of him. Several voices accompanied the footfalls. They moved too fast for him to make out any specific, precise word or piece of conversation. The only thing he was sure of was that the voices belonged to children, and somehow, they had run past without his catching a glimpse of them.

Craig squinted and looked southward down the sidewalk. An echo of the passing numerous feet was as audible as were the youthful voices.

An uneasy chill spread over Craig's limbs. He walked to the street side to check the sidewalk in both directions. But the sidewalk was empty, the street as well. He was alone except for the artificial illumination of the streetlights, the chirps of the crickets, and the music that continued to pulsate from an unknown household.

And the distant waning clops of running feet.

After several moments, they faded away completely. Craig was now aware of his own quick breathing.

*Only your imagination, stupid. If anyone had run by, you'd have seen them.*

He turned to walk back to the porch. This was when he noticed something in the yard to the left side of the flagstones.

The ground appeared to be entirely denuded of grass.

"What on earth?"

Craig looked about for some unknown light source responsible for the illusion. None of the neighbors had flipped on their porch lights; there was no change to the street lighting, no cars with headlights approaching. He peered up at the sky. But there were no beacons up there indicating a passing airplane or helicopter.

He looked back down, realizing now this portion of the yard was entirely covered by some material of a dull yellowish color and seemingly stony hard. He knelt for a closer look and stretched a hand over the ground where once there had been lush grass. Touching it, he found the texture rough and uneven.

Craig knew it was possible the landlady had ordered the grass to be limed and that he'd just not noticed it earlier.

*But why would Mrs. Delrutro have it limed?* he wondered. *And why just one side of the yard?*

Craig walked into the duplex and found a flashlight from a kitchen drawer. As he ventured back onto the porch, he aimed the flashlight at the part of the yard where he'd seen the material. He pushed the button that turned on the light. The illumination revealed what indeed appeared to be a mantle of limestone spread over the grass. And now Craig saw more details: here and there, across the limestone surface protruded what resembled clumps of twigs caked with dirt or maybe moss. Some of these clumps were dark, others somewhat beige in color. Craig walked onto the flagstones for a better look. He directed the illumination toward the nearest clump sticking out of the limestone, one rather tall and straggly in appearance.

His heart lurched in his chest.

This was no clump of vegetation but a human hand. The thing was small, knurled, and desiccated, like something out of a mummy exhibit. For a single shocked moment, Craig thought surely the thing belonged to some ancient corpse. With a trembling hand, he directed the flashlight toward another clump. He squinted at what it was he saw: another tiny hand.

Craig took an uncertain step onto the limestone. He directed the illumination of the flashlight here, there. With each turn he made, he saw some tiny cadaverous hand or digits jutting through the porous surface. Craig was dimly aware of how very fast his breathing had become, how his heartbeat thundered in his ears.

*An ungodly vision,* he told himself. *None of this is real!*

He made out something else at the edge of the limestone closest to the sidewalk –something that appeared fluffy and very tattered. Very carefully, he stepped around the multitude of mummified hands until he stood right in front of the object. Taking a deep breath, he directed the light directly onto whatever was wedged there. The fabric was moldy, but the faded plush fabric was still recognizable.

Tomato Head.

Craig remembered dreaming of Tomato Head. Yet, this was no dream. He was wide awake.

"I'm not asleep," he gasped. He turned away from the abominable thing and felt horrified tears scald his eyes.

A child's voice –no, numerous children's voices– whispered in the darkness, "You've been here before, Craig!"

For a moment, his heart seemed to stop beating. "*Go to hell!*" he roared. "Whoever you are doing this indecent thing, go to hell!"

Through misted eyes, he saw shadows lope across the yard on the other side of the walkway. A figure there stopped straight across from him. He could not see it, but he felt it. Hellishly black and emanating a phantom-like solidity that gave off a peculiar odor. Sweetly putrid, like flowers decaying in a vase.

He shone the light at the figure.

Betty Ann. She wore the same shorts and tee shirt as she had the first time he'd seen her. Her fair skin was the color of cream under the light; her blonde hair gleamed like golden ice.

"How the hell did you find out where I live?"

The guileless look on her face made Craig's blood

thicken. Shaking with rage, he strode over the walkway and grabbed her by the arms. How small and easily breakable those arms felt in his clenched hands. But he didn't care. He shook her and let loose a feral enraged yell.

His chest felt like it would explode. He could not breathe. His feet, his legs, and even his arms went numb. Black dots flickered before his eyes.

Craig perceived -but did not feel- his skull collide with the ground. The black dots scattered enough to allow a blurry view of the stars overhead. He snatched a thin gasp of air. Once, twice. He tried to sit up, but his head felt incredibly heavy, and the back of his skull hurt. With a helpless moan, he sank back to the ground.

Voices surrounded him. If these were passersby or neighbors, he could not tell. And though he opened his mouth and tried to ask for help, words would not vocalize. All he knew was the sensation of hands passing under his shoulders and of someone lifting his legs.

Dim waves passed through Craig's mind. He heard ordinary sounds from the inside of his house. His heart rate leveled out. The pain in his head lessened to a dull throb. And whoever it was that had carried him inside and laid him down had now gone.

How much time passed before he was able to move was only a guess. But eventually, his consciousness fought its way out of the dimness. He forced himself to sit up.

The throb in his head was nearly gone, though he felt a goose egg at the back of his head. The lamp by his bed had been turned on. Throwing his legs over the bedside, he noticed the beer bottle and flashlight standing on the table right beside the lamp. He had taken both these things outside. Of this, he was sure.

*But who carried me inside?*

He rose from the bed and stepped to the door. There

was no sign nor sound to suggest anyone else was in the house. Except for the lamp light from his room, the place appeared to be dark. He went back for the flashlight and switched it on.

"Hello?" he called into the living room. "Who is there?"

When no one answered, he did a walk-through of the entire house. The only other light he found on was the overhead in the kitchen. He was pretty sure the house had been this way right before he'd stepped out to the porch with the beer. Satisfied no one was about, he checked the back door. The French doors were locked, and the curtains closed shut. At length, he went to the front door.

The exterior light was still off, though the door remained open. *Or left open,* he thought.

Craig rubbed the tender spot on his skull. As he stared out into the darkness, he wondered if it was possible he'd just been drunk and fallen? That he'd imagined someone else putting himself in bed?

He cringed to recall what had happened in the yard. Surely, it couldn't have been real. He flipped on the switch for the porch light and walked out. With the flashlight illumination to guide him, he proceeded down the steps to the walkway. He took a deep breath and approached the dreaded part of the yard. He directed the flash over the spot.

Only grass covered the ground here. He knelt and fanned his fingers through it. Lush, dewy grass, and nothing else. He stood again and spread the light over the other side of the yard. This portion was normal, too. There was nothing amiss, not a thing.

Craig turned off the flashlight and went back into the house. After closing and locking the door, he returned to his room. He stood the flashlight atop the nightstand and picked up the beer bottle to check the weight.

It was practically full.

So he had not been drunk. He wanted to call Betty Ann

at the motel where she was staying. He wanted to hear her voice, to demand to know what she had done to him? Beg her, if he must, to just leave him alone. And if she laughed at him?

*I'll just end her sorry, useless life.*

Craig took his cell phone from the dresser and searched the internet search engine for the Relax-o-Lodge Inn. Almost instantly, a short description of the place popped up. There was a small photo of the inn, and as he touched this, he was led to a details and ratings web page. Below the street address, he found a phone listing for the office.

Craig touched the number link and held the phone to his ear. The call was answered after two rings.

"Relax-o-Lodge," a pleasant masculine voice spoke. "Wayne speaking. How may I help you?"

"I'm calling for one of your guests, Ms. Betty Ann Crawford. May I please have the phone number for her room?"

"One moment, sir, and I will look that up," Wayne said.

It was more like two hundred moments before Craig heard Wayne's voice again, "I apologize for the delay, sir. We don't get many extension requests these days, and I had to reacquaint myself with the system. If you hold, I will transfer your call now?"

"Yes, thank you, Wayne."

As Craig discerned a muted click on the line, his palms began to perspire. He was still angry –angrier than he'd ever been– and yet, he almost hoped Betty Ann would not pick up. For if she didn't, it most likely meant she was still en route from his place back to the inn. And such confirmation was the only kind he really wanted.

He heard a ring on the other end of the call. A second ring. A third. An abrupt pop as the call was picked up.

"Hello?" Betty Ann answered.

Craig knew what he wanted to say, but the words just wouldn't vocalize.

"Craig?"

His breath caught in his chest. *She is only guessing who this is,* he told himself firmly.

"Craig, I know this is you."

He took a deep, steadying breath. As it released, he hissed, "I don't know what your game is, Betty Ann. I don't care if you really are a medium. I don't even care if you take away the three-million-dollar prize. But if you ever come to my home again, if you screw with my head again, I will hurt you. Be very sure of that!"

There was a gentle sigh from the other end of the line. "You sound very upset," she said in a sympathetic voice. "Look, whatever you think, I am not the one responsible for what happened at your home. You need to look inside yourself, your life, if you want to find that out."

Craig bit back the scream of outrage that sprang to his lips. *The woman is insufferable!* With a punch of a forefinger, he pushed the button that ended the call. He tossed his phone to the end of the bed. For a few minutes, he expected Betty Ann to call back. He glared at the phone; his skin lathered in sweat. But no call came.

After a while, his tension began to subside. At the very least, he told himself, he'd managed to tell Betty Ann how he felt. His only regret was that he had not done it before now. He should have called Fred Wagoner's house before she'd left Tennessee and told her then exactly what he had told her tonight.

But it was enough for now. Tomorrow evening or the morning afterward, Betty Ann Crawford would be on a plane headed back to Tennessee. He returned his phone to the dresser. He set the alarm clock for 6 o'clock in the morning. It was quite a bit earlier than he typically got up, but he wanted to be at the studio before filming of the last challenge began.

He was smiling as he crawled into bed. Whatever perverse joy Betty Ann had taken in targeting him would be no more. He'd shown her he was not her plaything. And he was sure Pang's detective would discover the identity of whoever was helping her ever since she'd arrived in California.

He closed his eyes and fell into a restful slumber.

\*\*\*

In the morning, Craig drank three cups of coffee and took a shower before heading to the studio. It was just after seven o'clock when he pulled into the parking lot. Except for a few maintenance people, there was no one else to be found in the executive building. While waiting in his office alone, Craig sent Kesha a message asking how she was. After this, he shot one off to Heather to wish her a good morning, along with a reminder to call or message if she needed anything. At nearly seven-thirty, he heard someone come into the outer office. He wasn't sure if Matt or John was scheduled to work his outer office today. Either way, he really didn't want to engage in much conversation or concern himself with paperwork right now.

The outer phone rang, and Craig heard Matt answer it. The conversation was mostly a blur to his ears. But a moment later, Matt tapped at his door.

"Yes?"

Matt peeked his head in. "I thought you got here early. Saw your car in the lot."

"Yeah. I want to watch the taping for that Crawford woman's last challenge."

"Ah, her," Matt said. "Just got a call for you from the Relax-o-Lodge."

Craig was curious. With any luck, they were calling to say Betty Ann had checked out. It was very possible she had caught wind that Pang's detectives were hanging around the inn.

*Maybe,* he hoped, *she's already decided to head back to Tennessee.*

"What did they have to say?"

"It was the manager," Matt explained. "He says they are raising their prices for the coming year. But wants you to know they're giving us a twenty-five percent discount for any guests we book. If the studio signs a contract, that is."

Craig hid his disappointment with a laugh. "Our business bringing them up in the world, huh?"

"Appears so."

After Matt closed the door, Craig sat at his desk until a quarter till eight. At this time, he left the building and walked directly to the studio. Knowing where Agee was likely to be found at this hour of the morning, he made his way to the talent and wardrobe wing.

He entered the door, which opened to the small foyer close to the wardrobe department. There was a kitchen island here, and the coffee machine was making bubbling sounds as it brewed a fresh pot. Craig heard some of the wardrobe people talking from behind doors down the hallway. But he kept by the window near the main door and peered outside anxiously for Agee to appear. After just a minute or so, he saw the host approaching. Another man walked alongside him – some tanned, smartly dressed guy Craig did not know. As they reached the door, the two of them seemed to be arguing. Perhaps not exactly arguing, but it was apparent Agee was not happy. Before Agee opened the door, he made a dismissive gesture to the stranger. The man shrugged and turned while Agee entered the building.

The host slammed the door closed behind him. He was muttering under his breath as Craig stepped toward him.

"Was that the detective?" Craig asked.

Agee was momentarily taken off guard. "Oh, Craig!

Good morning. Yes, yes indeed it was."

"I hope he gave you an explanation as to why he didn't follow Betty Ann over to my place?"

Agee frowned. "What do you mean?"

"She was over at my place, Gerald. In my yard!"

Agee gestured for Craig to follow him. "My mind is running on only one cup of coffee right now. Let me grab another, and you come back to my wardrobe and explain what you mean. You're making no sense."

Craig felt an irritable chortle at the back of his throat. "He was supposed to keep an eye on the Crawford woman last night, right? Well, she showed up at my place, Gerald."

A couple of wardrobe women emerged from the hallway and stopped by the coffee maker. Agee tried again to coax Craig toward his wardrobe room.

"No!" Craig protested. "I want to know what that stupid detective was doing last night. Because he very obviously wasn't doing what he's supposedly paid to do."

He was aware the women were staring at them. One of them whispered something to the other. A moment later, they took their coffees outside. Agee had noticed them, too, and looked almost embarrassed.

The host scratched his head and eyed Craig incredulously. "But Craig, Mr. Kouris did exactly what he's paid to do. He, his wife, and their two electronic surveillance cameramen. That's what we were talking about when I arrived. I suppose you saw him outside?"

"Yes."

"Look, Kouris was told I needed every bit of information they gathered last night by this morning. They set up at a little after four yesterday afternoon. They had to cough up a pretty penny to pay off the people at the inn, but they got everything they needed: free access to the halls, the breakfast dining room, the pool room, and the laundry. Kouris and his people had surveillance film going on outside of the inn, too, both rear and front. They waited until the limo arrived to pick up the Crawford woman again this morning. And just a few minutes ago, I was sitting in Kouris's car. He showed me all their notes and the videos they took."

Craig sighed. "And?"

"They came away with nothing," Agee said. "Crawford stayed in her room all night."

"They're lying to you, Gerald. Betty Ann Crawford was over at my place last night."

Something akin to pity glinted in Agee's eyes. "You actually think you *saw* her?"

Craig felt the beginning of a headache. Seeing Betty Ann in his yard had seemed so real, but looking back, he wondered if he'd just envisioned her standing there before he fainted? It could have been that simple. But whether or not, he had no doubt that he'd spoken with her on the telephone.

"I think so, yes."

Agee grumbled. "*Think so* isn't much, you know? I'm sorry, but I just sat for over an hour watching all of Kouris's footage over fast-play. I read his team's notes. I talked to all of them. Crawford didn't come out of that room, Craig. She didn't even call room service. She never talked to anyone there." A sympathetic look softened Agee's features. "Believe me, no one wants to find out more than me who that woman has had helping her. We were just a little late, I suppose. But I promise we will keep digging. We will find out."

Craig couldn't believe what he was hearing. "No, no, this is unacceptable! She did talk to someone. She talked to me. I called her after she left my place and went back to the inn!"

Agee grimaced. "Now, why would you go and do that?"

Craig almost screamed out that Betty Ann had guessed

it was him on the phone. But no; even with Agee being the professional skeptic he was, Craig wouldn't take a chance on tainting his judgment during the last challenge. He knew it was paramount that Betty Ann was disgraced and disgraced with all professionalism intact.

He sighed. "You know, Gerald, it may have been just a stupid dream. I probably just drank too much before turning in."

"Craig, dear boy, don't let her get to you. We'll discover whoever her accomplice is. And between you, me, and the wall, there isn't a chance in all of hell I'll let that little piece of white trash get away with this."

"I hope you're right."

"I promise I am." Agee gave Craig's arm a good-natured clap. "Besides, I've tweaked the challenge for today. And I vow this time her fraud will be exposed!"

Craig was surprised. "You changed it? From the approved script?"

"Only slightly," Agee admitted. "I'm not using plants for it. I had no choice. Obviously, someone got a copy of the scripts for the other challenges in order to help her prepare. I don't know if it is my assistant or one of the production crew. It could be the make-up artist's errand boy, for all we know. But Barkley, Kraft, and I worked this one out over dinner last night. They are the only ones –besides you now– who know about this. And those two aren't about to leak it. They like the generous paychecks too well."

Craig saw the reason in what Agee planned. "Yeah, alright," he said. "You're the expert."

"Yes, I am," Agee chuckled. "Now stop worrying. I have to get ready for the taping. You going to watch from the control room?"

Craig nodded. Agee's plan did give him a great measure of relief.

"Good," Agee said. "You head on over to the control room. I have like twenty-five minutes to get my powder girl to do her magic and make me look ten years younger."

***

Craig arrived at the control room to find Vint, Danny, and Yvette already seated at the production desk. Another woman was there as well, sitting on a stool in front of the table where Vint kept his collection of bobbleheads. She was a gorgeous brunette and was dressed in a halter top and denim shorts. High-heeled sandals showed off her shapely bronze legs. Craig vaguely recalled Vint once introducing her as his fiancée. Hildy? Hope? Harvest? He knew it was something that started with *H*.

Danny greeted him with a little wave. Vint just nodded his head.

"Morning, Craig," Yvette said.

"Hi Craig, how are you?" asked the leggy gal.

"Good, good...*Harvest*, is it?"

The woman laughed. "Harmony."

Vint turned in his seat and said to her, "Okay darling, I don't care if you vape in here, but stay off your phone until we're done? If you just have to talk to someone, please step outside?"

"Of course, sweetie," Harmony replied. "I love you."

Vint blew her a kiss. "I love you, snookums."

Yvette shook her head with disgust. "You two. Geesh."

Danny grinned. "You're just jealous, Yvette."

"Hardly," Yvette countered. "I got my own man, more than can be said for you–"

"Quiet," Vint grumbled. He was looking at the monitors at the desk. "Looks like they're about to start."

Craig stepped up behind the three at the desk. From the image coming through the general viewing screen, he saw this challenge would take place in stage room C. It was the smallest, coziest of the stages. A wide table had been brought in and placed in the center of the floor. Barkley and Kraft were seated on one side of the table, and between them stood an unoccupied chair. Another empty chair had been placed on the other side of the table. From this set-up, Craig guessed multiple cameras were planned to be used for the filming.

The audio for the little surveillance monitor was turned off, but the screen was on. Through it, director Maisey Henderson and her film team were seen moving about the room as they finished their setup. A visual streaming through one of the monitor screens showed live footage from the team's main camera. This camera silently witnessed the left-hand stage door open. It was Agee. He paused and spoke with Maisey for a few moments before joining the other judges on their side of the table. Hal, a sound engineer assistant, approached Agee and affixed a small wireless microphone to the collar of his shirt. When Hal was satisfied, he also checked the microphones Barkley and Kraft wore.

The door opened again, and Katie Alberts came in with Betty Ann. Katie was dressed casually today, looking nothing like the glamorous hostess she had for the second challenge. She gestured for Betty Ann to take the lone seat across from the judges, and then she quickly darted out of the room.

"Goodness gracious," Vint snarked, "Katie must not want to stay."

"Can't say as I blame her," Danny said. "Considering last time."

Craig noticed Betty Ann was garbed today in a frumpy dark green prairie-style dress, her blonde hair pulled back in a single loose braid. Dressed in this way would have lent most women a decidedly homespun appearance, and Craig suspected Agee had personally arranged this detail with the wardrobe people. Deliberate downplaying of a woman's looks was a trick long used in television, as it was believed to play on the psyche of the audience and give them the impression the woman was dour, unsophisticated, and/or less educated than her peers. But if this indeed was what Agee planned, Craig had to admit it failed. Betty Ann looked as intelligent and pleasingly sincere to the eye as ever.

As Hal affixed a mic to Betty Ann's dress, Craig noticed her idly finger something hanging at her wrist. It took a moment before Craig recognized it as the same seashell pasta bracelet he had seen her wearing in Tennessee. He was reminded of Fred Wagoner and all the gullible old people she'd duped back in Tennessee. For an instant, he felt a sliver of the same rage he had known the night before. But he managed to stifle the urge to dwell on this feeling and instead concentrated on Agee's assurance that none of Betty Ann's tricks would work today.

One boom operator stationed himself as discreetly as possible behind the judges. The other did the same behind Betty Ann. The rest of the film crew moved close against the inner wall, out of shot from the cameras. The crew would be unseen by the control room monitors and just barely noticeable through the surveillance camera.

Maisey Henderson stepped in front of the surveillance camera and passed a palm in front of her face. Danny responded by flipping the audio switches on.

Vint punched a couple of buttons on the desk. With a soft hiss of electronic buzz, blank screens popped up on two monitors. Yvette put on her headset and turned it on.

Now Vint pushed the button for the between-room conference. "We're ready, Maisey."

Maisey called the crew to *roll*, and with a signal from her cameraman, she receded from view. The cameramen acknowledged they were ready. A moment later, live feed began streaming from their cameras and through the two active desk monitors.

A loud *snap!* was heard from the slate of the clapperboard.

"Cameras set," Maisey announced.

She must have motioned to Agee. For now, he raised his chin to look into the camera directed at the judges and began his dialog.

"Welcome back to The Debunker's Challenge," he said. "So far this week, guest Betty Ann Crawford has undergone a series of wholly unbiased and scientifically principled appraisal challenge tests in an effort to prove her medium abilities. This will be the third and final challenge. After we are done here, our judges will convene in order to apprise all three of Betty Ann's performances. And, if we are convinced of her powers, she will be awarded the three-million-dollar prize."

Agee gave a little nod to his fellow judges and bestowed Betty Ann a stoic look. Craig saw that as adeptly as Agee hid his emotions, Barkley was a different story. Her lips were drawn in a sharp, simpering smile while darts downright danced in her eyes. By contrast, Craig thought Kraft appeared not only relaxed but in a very good mood. In fact, there seemed to be something akin to either admiration or fondness in the way he looked at Betty Ann.

"Hello again, Betty Ann," Agee said. "Are you ready to begin?"

At her nod, Agee continued, "Good, good. For today's challenge, we have designed something that involves a certain level of risk for the judges. The risk is not physical but one where we are willing to allow some of our most personal life events to be made public. This is Betty Ann, if you are able to tell us what these life events are. We have chosen this particular challenge as it occurred to us there is a possibility an insider has taken it upon themselves to help you. And by help, I mean feeding you information they were not permitted to share."

The camera aimed at Betty Ann showed a slight purse to her lips.

"Of course," she replied.

"Ms. Crawford," Barkley said, "You don't seem surprised."

"Why should I be?"

Barkley's tongue flicked cat-like over her upper lip, but she was content to say nothing more just yet.

"This is a good thing, I must suppose," Agee said. He looked at Barkley and Kraft. "Don't you both agree?"

Barkley nodded, and Kraft smiled blandly.

Agee reached into his shirt pocket and pulled out an envelope. Kraft drew out an identical envelope from his own shirt pocket while Barkley removed one from a pocket at the front of her blazer. The judges placed these envelopes on the table in front of them.

"Betty Ann," Agee explained, "inside these envelopes, you see are sheets of paper. Each of us has written out a statement on our respective papers. These statements briefly detail single events, events that have occurred in our personal lives, events which, until now, have never been shared with the public. Additionally, we have each put our signatures to our statements for validation purposes. You are asked to disclose what is written in our statements. After you tell us what you believe the first judge's statement reads, their envelope will be opened. The written statement will be revealed to the camera person filming behind us, and the judge will read it out loud. After this, you will move on to the second judge in the same manner and then the third judge. Is this clear for you?"

Betty Ann folded her hands together atop the table. "Yes, it is clear."

Craig noticed a fierce flicker in Betty Ann's eyes, and there was a subtle yet notable strain in her serene composure.

He felt happy about this, as it indicated to him that Betty Ann wasn't feeling as confident with this challenge as she had been with the others.

Danny must have seen it, too, for he commented, "Your little medium looks a little tense, Craig."

From the stage room, Agee spoke like a diplomat, "Alright. And in the spirit of fairness, Ms. Crawford, you may choose whichever statement you wish to start with. After you have told us about the first one and the statement has been revealed, you are good to go to the next. Does this sound fair to you?"

Betty Ann only nodded. Agee made an amicable gesture and told her, "Then you may start as soon as you're ready."

The camera leveled on Betty Ann showed her eyes move momentarily from one envelope to another. Her eyes settled on Agee.

"Mr. Agee," she said, "your statement regards a dog. You wrote that you had this dog when you were young. You tell us his name was King, a red setter-hound mix and your best childhood friend. You further write that one day, you took King along when you went to fish at a local stream. King waded into the water and stuck his nose under the surface as if hunting for something. He pulled out a brown trout and laid it on the bank near you. He proceeded to catch two more brown trout. You write that not only were you amazed by King's success, but his obvious happiness over it was contagious. You mark it down as one of the happiest days of your young life."

Agee was smiling, though Craig guessed it was a poker smile. The host reached for his envelope and tore open one end. He pulled out a sheet of cream-colored stationery and unfolding it, laid it over the table. The cameraman, with his boom, directed the camera so that it revealed what was written there.

Agee read aloud the statement he'd written, *"When I was about fourteen, I took my red setter hound King fishing with me to a nearby stream. While I sat there using my old pole and some fresh worms, King waded into the stream. He was excited by the fish darting in the clear water. To my delight, King pulled out three of the fish with only his teeth. He brought his prizes one by one up to the bank where I sat and deposited them at my feet. They appeared to be brown trout. King was so thrilled by what he'd done, and I was overjoyed for him. I recall that day as one of the happiest of my life."*

Agee looked to Betty Ann and remarked in a cool tone, "I must concede that on the surface, your guess does surprise me."

Kraft threw him an incredulous look. "I'd call it a rather impressive *guess*."

Barkley sniffed and shook her head. "Well, you are easily impressed, Zane."

In the control room, Craig was distracted by a waft of fruity aroma. A curl of light mist swirled around his right shoulder. Casting a look that way, he saw mist coming from Harmony puffing on a slender vape. He smiled faintly and looked back at the monitors.

Agee was just saying, "Alright, Betty Ann, who is next?"

Betty Ann turned her attention to Barkley. "Dr. Barkley," she said, "you have written about the first time you kissed a boy. You were sixteen years old. It took place during a trip taken by your school band to Six Flags Over Texas. The boy's name was Scott Hannity. He was a senior, and while you considered him a real nerd, you secretly thought he was very cute, too. A month after this, Scott asked you to go to the prom. But your parents wouldn't let you because–"

"Hold on!" Barkley blurted out. "That's enough!" She crossed her arms tightly and shot Agee an indignant glare.

"Am I right, Dr. Barkley?" Betty Ann asked.

After several tense moments, Barkley tore one end of her envelope and drew out a sheet of stationery. The cameraman focused in on the words written there. Barkley grabbed the glass of water nearby and took a deep sip before looking at the text. There was a notable tremor in her voice as she finally read aloud, "*When I was sixteen, I went with the school band to Six Flags Over Texas. A boy named Scott Hannity sat on the bench beside me. Although Scott was a nerd, and most of my friends didn't even know who he was, I always thought he was as cute as he was smart. During the trip to the amusement park, we got a chance to talk. Then, about an hour into the drive, while nobody else was looking, Scott reached over and kissed me. It was the first real kiss of my life.*"

"That was certainly interesting," Kraft said.

Barkley shot a glance toward the main camera, her mouth drawn tightly. "Yeah, alright," she said with a dismissive motion. "Move along."

At the production desk, Danny asked, "Anyone else get the feeling Betty Ann was about to reveal more than Barkley had written in her statement?"

"The doc did seem anxious to interrupt her," Vint granted.

In the studio, the judges were now engaged in some light-hearted banter. Craig didn't catch what they were saying as he was suddenly distracted by a sound. It was a tic-tock sound and seemed to be coming from the table where Vint kept all his bobble toys. For an instant, he thought it had to be a running clock positioned on the wall. But then he was sure it was a double tic-tock he was hearing. He saw Harmony standing by the table and, raising his eyes, realized there was no clock on the wall.

*Tic-tock, tic-tock, tic-tock!*

He glanced curiously over the other walls. There had

to be a clock somewhere, even if he didn't remember where.

"They've got minds of their own today, huh?" he heard Harmony say.

"Huh?"

She gestured to something on the table. "Those silly toys. Minds of their own."

Craig's eyes pored over Vint's collection. There, among the new and the classic figures, two of the bobblehead figures were moving. One of the figures was a little flower sitting in a green pot. It was, in fact, a plastic daisy with a smiley-face disk haloed by white fabric petals. Beside this bobblehead sat a cube of smooth wood with a metal spring inserted vertically into the center. The little spring held up a wooden placard – shaped and painted like a rainbow, with glittery sparkles all over it. The daisy bobblehead gyrated in its plastic pot while the wooden rainbow swayed back and forth atop its quick-weaving spring. Craig stared, transfixed by the motion of the bobbles. For a few moments, he didn't quite understand why he found the bobbles so fascinating.

Then suddenly, he recalled something Betty Ann had said to him that evening in Tennessee: *When the daisy dances with the rainbow, you will learn where Kristophe is.*

A sense of trepidation fell over Craig. It was as if some invisible entity had slinked into the room, and its unseen presence infused the air and pervaded the very pores of his flesh. He knew the feeling was irrational. Yet it was so vivid, so intense. He flinched and felt his front teeth slice into his bottom lip.

"Hey Craig, you alright?"

It was Harmony. Concern shone in her wide eyes.

Craig couldn't answer; he couldn't even make himself nod. He forced himself away from the table and went to stand beside Vint. Taking a deep breath, he wiped away the trickle of blood that streamed down his chin. His eyes moved to the monitors. Only now did he realize the judges' banter had taken on a testy tone. He had missed the last comments made in the stage room, but he could tell by the way Barkley looked at Agee that she was irate.

Agee said, "Protest as you want, Leslie. But I believe there is a credible reason for doubt."

"We can discuss this later, Gerald," Barkley grunted.

Craig saw Agee's jaw clench.

*He thinks she's the one colluding with Betty Ann,* Craig thought.

Agee gestured to their guest. "Betty Ann, you might as well continue."

Betty Ann turned her attention to Zane Kraft. Her gaze was soft, nearly sad, as she regarded him.

"Mr. Kraft, you write that someone you recently had contact with has disappeared. You want me to tell you what has happened to him? You ask where he can be found. You also state you feel finding this out is much more important than ratings for this show."

Barkley frowned in evident confusion. She glanced at Agee, who only looked impassively from Betty Ann to Kraft.

Kraft took a deep breath and opened his envelope. He laid his statement to the table, and the camera focused in on his handwritten words as he read it.

*"Someone I recently met has gone missing. Although in this, I ask you to tell us something not agreed to by the rules of this challenge, if you can, please tell us this individual's location? Finding this person is much more important than getting good ratings for a mere television show."*

A very audible scoff broke Agee's stoic demeanor. "Zane," he asked, "you didn't happen to talk with Ms. Crawford before we gathered in this room, did you?"

A wounded look crossed Kraft's face, but it was Barkley who said, "For god's sake, Gerald. Moments ago, you insinuated practically the same thing about me! Are you trying to say the two of us got together and collaborated with Ms. Crawford?"

Agee offered a curmudgeonly reply, "As a lifelong student of human behavior, no behavior surprises me."

Barkley's face beamed red. "Need I remind you I am a licensed and trained specialist in human behavior?"

From her seat at the production desk, Yvette muttered, "This is getting ugly."

Craig fully expected the tension in the studio would compel Maisey to call a break in filming. At this point it was the only professional decision to make. He was also still keenly aware of the tic-tocking from the dancing bobbleheads. The incessant sound felt like a screwdriver plowing through his temple.

In the studio, Kraft ignored Agee. "Betty Ann," he implored, "will you tell me? Tell us? Please?"

Betty Ann shot an impatient glance at the camera, filming her reactions. At last, she said, "Mr. Kraft, the one you are concerned about is not far. Neither is he alone. Close by are companions he cannot see."

Agee made an exasperated look but he said nothing. Barkley appeared mesmerized. And Craig felt perspiration erupt over every inch of his flesh.

"Their names are unknown to you," Betty Ann told Kraft calmly. "But they call out to be remembered. Some of them have gathered from long distances away, from places you have probably never heard of. Those who were taken from places in this vicinity will be found very close to the one you seek. Their names are: Evan Osteen. Brian Cho. Nicolas Leyman. Peyton Hemmer. Adam Pyle. Noah Garcia. Kristophe Herbert."

Silent thunder quaked Craig's insides. He was vaguely aware of the shocked look Vint shot him and how ashen

Danny's face turned.

"Craig," Danny asked, "Kristophe Herbert...isn't that your little brother's name?"

But Craig could only stare at the monitors in breathless anticipation. He saw Agee shake his head and gesture to Maisey.

"This is inappropriate, Maisey," Agee bellowed. "Stop filming."

Maisey must have disagreed because the cameras continued to film. Betty Ann addressed Kraft again, "These I have named lie beneath a blanket of hardened limestone. The others will be found elsewhere."

Agee turned in his seat and smacked the camera of the boom operator standing behind him. The surprised man took a step back as Agee announced, "This deceitful woman is trying to get the network sued! Turn the cameras off!"

Maisey finally relented and ordered the cameramen to stop filming.

Yvette pulled off her headset. But via the surveillance monitor and its audio, those in the production room continued to witness what transpired in the stage room.

Kraft wiped his mouth nervously. "Betty Ann, is Brent Price alive?"

Agee shook his stony face and crossed his arms. "They've stopped filming. You two can end this charade now."

Betty Ann ignored him as she addressed Kraft, "Yes, Mr. Kraft, but Brent is injured. His abductor took him to his own house and, after drugging him, led him to a small room in the basement. There, Brent put up a fight and managed to elude his abductor by taking refuge in a small crawlspace behind a water heater. The abductor is not as small as Brent, and so cannot reach him. So this man decided to just lock the basement door. As the basement is well insulated, the boy's screams for help have gone unheard."

Craig bit his bottom lip again, and his fingernails clawed into the back of Vint's chair. He heard Harmony ask in a frightened voice if what was happening in the stage room was real?

Desperate tears shone in Kraft's eyes. "Whose house, Betty Ann? *Whose?*"

Just as Craig was sure his legs would buckle, Betty Ann's face glowed pale. "The only person here cold-blooded enough to have killed his own mother. Who burned her house down afterward and assumed another name. One who traveled far and wide working as first a circus carny, then a band roadie before he found himself lucky enough to be taken under the wing of a stage telepathist. The same person who escaped drug and sexual crime charges when he accepted a federal deal to help expose a securities fraud scheme...a second deal for infiltrating a notorious drug cartel. A man who has proved so valuable to government agents that they turned a blind eye to his molestation of little boys. The person who has not just molested children but one who spent decades killing victims throughout seven different states. One who has elite, wealthy friends who have perversely and directly benefited from his knowledge of how to lure unsuspecting children."

Betty Ann's eyes now leveled on Agee. "The one who wrote about a dog he never owned and who has never cast a fishing pole in his life."

Barkley gasped and covered her mouth.

Agee glared at the doctor. "She's lying, you stupid cow!"

Kraft was incredulous. "Betty-Betty Ann, are you serious?"

"You will find Brent in his basement," she told Kraft. "And the bodies of those children I named. Contact your local authorities. Contact them now."

Betty Ann's voice echoed in Craig's head. The words felt like the memory of a shadow, something he'd dreamed she had said to him: *You've been here before.* Without his even trying, another memory flooded back. A visit he'd once made to Agee's house. He had gone there to discuss some trivial matter about a potential guest. And while he was there Agee had invited him to follow him to the basement to get a couple of soda pops from the vintage machine kept there. There was something else stored down there, too, something so common that Craig had forgotten it until now. A water heater.

He saw Agee shoot up from his stage room chair. The host tore the mic off his shirt and threw it to the table. "I am not listening to any more of this!"

As Betty Ann spoke next, she repeated something Agee had said to Craig in private, "*Train yourself to see people as mere smoke, and in time, you can forget anyone's face.*"

Agee recoiled so hard that every muscle in his face twisted. Craig knew now that despite whatever logic and reason and Agee's irate reaction argued, Betty Ann spoke the truth.

The hatred he'd harbored toward Betty Ann vanished, replaced by a sense of stark and absolute lucidity.

He watched as the host moved from the table. Agee stormed briskly toward the wing door.

"Agee's intending to leave!" Danny shouted. "From that side of the building!"

"And no one in there will move to stop him," Craig hissed.

Vint looked at Harmony. "Quick, give me your phone!"

Just as Agee stamped toward the stage room exit, Craig turned and propelled through the control room door. He turned left and sprinted down the corridor, threw open the door there at the end. The daylight was blinding, but he ignored it and let familiarity lead him down the sidewalk. His running strides brought him to the studio parking lot and to the designated spot where Agee always parked.

The host had just reached his orange Jaguar coupe. He pulled the remote keyless system from his pants pocket and aimed it at the car. Craig heard a little *bing!* as the mechanism responded and the doors unlocked.

"Twenty-five hundred dollars of *charity*, Gerald," Craig shouted. "That's how much you paid to gain that poor, sick boy's trust!"

Agee looked at him, his face red with irritation. "Oh dear lord, Craig. Don't tell me you give any credence to that charlatan!"

Craig lunged forward. He grasped the host's belt with one hand, snatched his collar with the other, and shoved Agee's forehead into the side of the Jaguar. The impact made an ugly thud. Craig forcefully spun Agee around and, grabbing the man's shoulders, pinned him against the metal.

Blood trickled from a wound over the bridge of Agee's nose. He threw up his hands defensively, and Craig realized he'd never seen the man look so honestly his age. Absent was the imperious aplomb, the conceited glow. He was nothing more than a trembling, bleeding old man. And as strong as Craig's urge was just to break his scrawny neck, he had to think of Brent Price.

"Gerald, I should kill you now," he said. "But we're going to call the police instead. You're going to take them to your house, to the basement."

"Listen to yourself," Agee stammered. "You can't believe some damned Appalachian hill witch!"

A frosty chortle rose in Craig's throat. "Classic Gerald Agee. Denigrate someone in your high and mighty voice of reason and expect the rest of the world to dismiss them as liars and charlatans!"

Agee grunted and writhed like a worm to free himself.

Craig raised a hand and struck Agee so hard across the mouth that the back of the host's head banged into the car.

"Everyone in that studio knows," Craig growled. "We have the tape. We are going to call the police, and you are going to take them to Brent Price, master psychic debunker."

The mockery must have struck a nerve, for now, Agee sneered, "Do you have any idea who really controls the Debunker's Challenge? Who owns this studio? Who manages the whole damned network? They are my associates. MY patrons, Craig. And let me warn you, none of us take orders from some mediocre, easily replaceable field producer."

"Let your precious Worldwide Reason Institute do what they want!" Craig roared. "But it will have to wait until Brent is found. Even if that means I strangle you here and now and then tell the police where they can find that boy."

"If Brent Price is at my house," Agee seethed, "it's only because he came to me willingly!"

Craig's hands clamped around Agee's throat. His voice was hoarse as he asked, "Even my little brother, you depraved bastard?"

Feral contempt burned in Agee's eyes. "They *all* come to me willingly."

Craig's restraint snapped. His fingers dug into the host's wiry throat. Agee squirmed for breath; his hands flailed impotently at Craig's face. Craig smiled at the look of utter disbelief that shone in the old degenerate's eyes. As his grasp tightened over Agee's windpipe, the host managed to sputter a single unintelligible plea. But Craig did not hear it, only the *tic-tock* sound that resounded in his head. He was not even aware when, the next moment, a pair of security guards ran up to them.

The two grabbed Craig's forearms and wrenched him off Agee. As they held Craig back, Agee crumbled to the pavement, gasping for air.

*"Wrong guy!"* The shout had come from Vint. He and Danny sprinted toward them.

Vint pointed at Agee. "That's the one we called about!"

The guards exchanged confused looks. But they released Craig, and Danny helped Craig to his feet.

"It's okay, man," Danny said. "I contacted the CBI while Vint called these guys."

Craig nodded mutely. At last, the tic-tocking sound began to fade away. He saw one of the guards speaking to somebody over a cell phone. The other guard crouched beside Agee, who was holding his bruised throat.

"Try not to move, sir," the guard told him. We're contacting 9-1-1."

Agee's only response was a blubbering wail.

# CHAPTER EIGHT

In a police station interview room, Craig had provided two officers with his version of the incident at the studio lot and the events leading up to it. He'd told them everything, leaving nothing out. He also let them know he wasn't sorry. And most importantly, he urged them to check out the basement of Agee's home.

That had been almost three hours earlier. Now, at last, the door opened again. Sgt. Valdez, who had been one of the officers he had spoken with, entered with another man in plainclothes. The man introduced himself as Detective Mitchell Drummond.

To Craig's surprise, the detective informed him they had no charges to file against him.

"Not unless that Agee guy decides differently in the next forty-eight hours," Drummond added. "But I think Mr. Agee has more to worry about right now."

"What about the boy?" Craig asked anxiously, "Brent Price?"

"Your co-workers confirmed what you told us," Valdez said. "They showed us the tape you spoke of. We watched it with agents from the California Bureau of Investigations. Afterward, the agents went directly to Agee's home. As this involved a child and they felt there were adequate reasons to warrant a search based on immediate danger, they entered

the premises. About thirty minutes ago, they contacted us
with confirmation they had discovered Brent Price alive in the
basement. That woman was right, Mr. Herbert. The boy was
hiding in a crawlspace behind the water heater. Very small
opening, barely more than a crevice. The boy is dehydrated
and hungry. But the agents told us he was en route to the
hospital, and his mother has been contacted in Red Bluff."

A wave of relief washed over Craig. "Where is Agee?"

"He's in transport now from the emergency room,"
Valdez said.

"And the bodies said are under the limestone?"

Valdez's voice was reassuring as he said, "Agents are
breaking the limestone floor even as we speak, Mr. Herbert. I
cannot promise what they will find, if anything."

Drummond took a chair beside Craig. "I hate to have
to ask this, but are you sure this Betty Ann Crawford did not
know Gerald Agee before she came here?"

"No. She had never met him." Craig sighed. "And until
today, I believed she was a fraud. Agee was sure she was. But
she is no fraud. For that, I owe her an apology. More than an
apology. So much more than an apology, you know?"

There was a brief silence in the room. At length,
Drummond explained they would be in contact with Craig as
soon as they heard anything else from the CBI.

"CBI is arranging to extend Ms. Crawford's stay at the
Relax-o-Lodge," Drummond said. "For although everything
she has told us has been supported by the witnesses and the
videotapes, investigators will have more questions for her."

Craig walked out of the interrogation room to find
Matt in the station's waiting room. Matt explained Danny had
informed him of what had gone down at the studio. He said
he'd come down to either find out if Craig needed him to call
a lawyer or to drive him home.

During the drive, Matt didn't say anything more.

But once they arrived at Craig's place, Matt told him sympathetically, "It is an awful thing, Craig. I don't know whether to give my condolences or keep praying Kristophe is alive and well."

Craig nodded mutely and thanked him. Once inside the duplex, he felt the crushing weight of the feelings he held toward Agee. It was a mixture of immeasurable hatred and disgust, so cold and intense that it numbed his other emotions. But he felt absolutely no regret for attacking Agee. And he knew if the lowlife committed suicide in jail or was killed by another inmate, the world would be better off.

And yet Craig couldn't help but wonder why he had never once suspected Agee? Why had he never even got a whiff of the guy's perversity? Why had he never felt any hint there was something disturbing and unnatural about him?

He took a shower –hotter and longer than usual– and afterward called Kesha. Without going into details (which he knew would likely hit the news soon enough), he explained she should return home the next day.

"Are you alright?" Kesha asked.

"Yes. But something has happened."

He heard her take a deep breath. "Is it about Kristophe? Has he been found?"

He choked back an unexpected sob. "We may have news very soon. And I need you here."

Kesha said she would tell her friends at once. She told him she loved him, and the call ended.

He was just about to call Heather as well when a knock sounded at the front door. It was Heather. Her eyes were red from crying, and the wretched look on her face told him that she already knew what had happened.

"Matt called me," she explained. "He picked me up and dropped me by. I am so sorry, Craig!"

She threw her arms around him. Her tenderness

shattered the strange numbness which had encased Craig since the security guards pulled him off of Agee. For a long while, they stood in the open doorway, Heather holding him while he wept.

Heather stayed with him all that night. She even slept in the bed beside him. His sleep was deep, without dreams, without visions. He might have slept even longer had she not roused him early to say Detective Drummond had reached his cell phone.

When he answered the call, Drummond explained that CBI agents were on their way to the police station and that they had asked Craig to come in to look at some video.

Drummond offered to drive over and pick him up.

Forty minutes later, he and Heather were escorted by Drummond into a small, rather cozy room at the station. There was a couch here, along with a beverage cooler and snack machine. California Bureau of Investigations Agent Eileen Robards was here, too. Her voice was professional, though her tone was distinctively warm. As she gestured for them to have a seat, Craig noticed a large, soft leather briefcase at the end of the couch.

Robards explained that the CBI had worked throughout the night to excavate Agee's basement and that they had focused their work on the limestone floor near the hiding place where Brent Price had been found. The agent had brought some images from what they had found so far.

She reached for the briefcase and, opening it, took out a digital camera. "We have not yet located every family we need to speak with," Robards said, taking a seat beside Craig. "Nor have we yet converted all these digital images to physical photographs. We do, however, have the missing person's report details made when your brother disappeared, along with the report, the photos you provided at the time, the eyewitness statements taken from your former housekeeper, and so forth. So, we have a detailed description of what Kristophe was wearing that day. If you think you can, Mr. Herbert, would you please take a look at a couple of these images? They were taken at the excavation site in Mr. Agee's residence."

At his nod, she brought up an image gallery on the camera. Then she warned him to brace himself, as the images were disturbing.

"Let me tap the first one," she said, "take a look at this one, and we will then move on to the others, okay?"

She handed him the camera. As he looked at the display, she tapped the key that brought up an image. It was a photo of something in a ratty plastic bag laid atop broken flooring inside Agee's basement. But the next series of photos were particularly horrific: the bag had been drawn off the contents, revealing a single small body. The body lay on one side in a fetal position. It was mummified, and the hair that clung to the scalp had turned to an ashen shade of orange. The clothing was considerably faded, but Craig recognized the cheerful zigzag pattern on the quarter-length shirt. He knew those blue jeans – he had hemmed them with his mother's old sewing machine because the legs had been so long. There were no shoes on the body, just little white crew socks. And clutched close to the dead child's arms, right against the breastbone, was the plush Tomato Head, which Kristophe had loved so well.

Craig's heart sank, and his limbs quaked. "It's my brother Kristophe."

"You are absolutely certain?"

He tried to utter an answer, but all he could do was mouth *yes!*

To his relief, Robards turned the camera off and put it away again.

"That is all I need, sir," she said apologetically. "I am

so very sorry for your loss."

A disturbing question rose to Craig's mind. He did not want to ask it, but he had to. "Have you any idea how my brother…was killed?"

Robards bit her bottom lip as if reluctant to answer. At length, she said, "We cannot be sure yet. But we did find a horde of drugs inside the house. Most of them are very strong sedatives."

She told him Kristophe's body would be taken to the CBI's forensics office for a complete autopsy. She also let him know the remains of seven other children had been recovered from the basement.

"Ms. Crawford has given us names," she said. "The same ones she named in front of the studio cameras. We are in contact with the presumed families."

Craig remembered something. "And the others? She alluded that there were more."

Robards nodded. "Yes. She is providing the names of those as well. The locations where she believes they are buried. We have contacted the FBI. They will be initiating their own investigations on those. If those names pan out, the FBI will be in contact with authorities in the respective States in which she says the victims died."

Craig's whole body shuddered with rage and grief. He was so grateful to feel Heather's steady hands on his arm.

"I am very sorry for having to put you through this," Robards said. "And I thank you for coming in today. I, or someone in my office, will contact you to let you know when you and your family can claim Kristophe for burial. And on behalf of everyone at the Bureau, I extend my deepest condolences."

Heather offered to stay at the duplex with him, and Craig was relieved to have her there. At a little after three that afternoon, Zoe's car pulled into the driveway. From a window, Craig saw Kesha step out of the vehicle. He went out and helped carry her bags into the house.

Only once they were inside did Kesha say anything, and this she uttered in a shaky half-whisper. "Tell me, what have you heard?"

Heather excused herself while the two of them talked on the sofa. It was not the happy ending story either of them had always prayed to hear. It was ugly. It was enraging. Once Craig had finished and Kesha knew everything, they were both sobbing. But she took his hand, kissed it, and laid it over her heart.

"He's at rest, brother," she said, the tears spilling down her face. "And at the very least, now we know. Just promise me you will not blame yourself."

Kesha knew him so well. But he did blame himself. Not once in all these years had he ever suspected anyone he knew of being monstrous enough to take a child, and certainly not the kind of monster who would kill a child. He believed firmly now that had he been smart, or at least in tune with his perceptions, then somewhere down the line, he would have picked up some kind of misgiving or hint about Agee's nature.

"I should have had some sense about Agee," he said miserably. "You'd think that, right? We are human beings. We have instinct. But I didn't pick up on anything. Not once in all these years. And here I thought I knew that man."

Kesha was thoughtful. At length, she said, "That is the secondary evil in all this, Craig. A person like Agee commits unthinkable acts, and gets away with it because he excels at deception. People like this not only labor to satisfy and cover up their wickedness, they corrupt their every relationship with their falsehoods. If he wasn't so very contemptible, so very evil, one might even feel sorry for such a lonesome individual."

She wiped her tears away with the back of a hand. "But don't you dare take the blame for what Agee's done," she warned firmly. "He has already injured this family; I don't want to see him using your conscience to carry his blame. Whatever you do, Craig, make him shoulder the responsibility. One hundred percent of it!"

\*\*\*

Over the next few days, news outlets were saturated with headlines about Brent Price's rescue and the discovery of bodies at Agee's home. The local District Attorney's office charged Agee with felony imprisonment, child exploitation, molestation, and illegal disposal of corpses. Federal murder and kidnapping indictments also loomed over Agee's future.

Because of the host's celebrity and legion of groupies, social media was hit by a firestorm of controversy. While most ordinary people were shocked and outraged, Agee's fans were indignant. His long-time mainstream media supporters depicted Agee as an educated, sympathetic old man. Progressive pundits, blog posters, and video personalities vehemently defended him and alluded that he had been set up. Although Brent Price's age kept his name from being published, these defenders argued that the "alleged" kidnapping victim must have been a willing visitor to Agee's home. They decried the evidence recorded on the studio tapes as unreliable. A few went so far as to put forth the theory that the discovered corpses had been placed in Agee's home by charlatans who had been exposed on The Debunker's Challenge. These conspiracy theorists angrily maintained any legitimacy, given the ordeal by legal authorities stemmed from an agenda crafted against the entire skeptic community. Their favorite debunker was a victim, they maintained, singled out by a cabal of ignorant, superstitious people with a grudge against science and reason.

Jon gave Craig the heads up that the network was talking

about shelving production of The Debunker's Challenge until further notice. Craig also learned Betty Ann was interviewed several times by both State and Federal agents. But after ten days, they were satisfied she had no previous relationship with Agee that could tie her in with his crimes. She did, however, provide the names and locations of the numerous victims she asserted waited outside of California. The FBI moved quickly to begin investigations and recovery of bodies in these other locales.

One morning, Craig was in the kitchen when he heard a knock at the front door. Kesha was back at school, and Heather was still asleep, and though Craig wasn't expecting a visitor, he opened the door. To his surprise, he found Walter Pang standing on the porch. Pang held a smart leather briefcase in his hand, and his dress shirt was slightly damp from perspiration. In every other way, however, the attorney stood there as coolly poised as usual.

Craig asked him inside. Pang offered a condolence before accepting the offer to sit down on the sofa. Craig was still trying to get used to condolences. He could only reply with a nod and asked Pang if he could get him a beverage?

"Oh, no thank you, Craig."

Craig took a seat in the old wing-back chair across from the coffee table. "So, what brings you out this way, Mr. Pang?"

Pang opened the briefcase over his lap. "I do not know if either of your assistants contacted you to inform you, Craig, but this morning, the network executives decided to cancel The Debunker's Challenge."

Craig found the news darkly amusing. "Really? Well, what a shame."

"It is reasonable, considering the circumstances," Pang said. "The studio has openings for the crew, so you need not worry about them having to look for work. And your assistants have been accepted into the studio's secretarial pool, so they will be put into new positions soon enough."

Craig told Pang he was glad to hear this. But he admitted he wasn't surprised by the network's decision.

"I can assure you, Craig, it did not come with any cheer. But I know you understand a network cannot ethically continue with a series created by a dissolute person. To do any business with such an individual would be irresponsible."

"I know," Craig replied. "And Gerald Agee *was* The Debunker Challenge."

"Yes. But please know the network extends its deepest regrets to you and your family in this time of tragedy. It is for this they have asked me to come by." Pang pulled a sealed business envelope out of the briefcase. "The network feels it is their obligation to offer what assistance they may to our company employees who have suffered because of Mr. Agee's actions."

He laid the envelope on the coffee table. "This cannot possibly replace your family's loss, Craig, but we hope it will help ease the burden."

Craig reached tentatively for the envelope. He opened it and peeked at the cheque tucked inside. He'd never seen so many zeros written out to his name.

Although Craig knew he should be grateful, there was something undeniably artificial about this seeming act of generosity. He remembered when Pang had informed him the network had nixed Brent's episode on the heels of his disappearance. At the time, the CEOs wanted to avoid scandal out of fear. Brent's failure to take home the prize money made him depressed enough to run away from home. Craig was doubtless these same powerful people now feared he and Kesha might blame them for Kristophe's kidnapping and death.

"This is more than a mere severance cheque," Craig

said stiffly. "Am I right to suspect your bosses are afraid I will bring a lawsuit against the studio? That they want to buy me off?"

Pang rolled his tongue behind his bottom lip and said in a diplomatic manner, "Whatever for? The network is not responsible for Gerald Agee's actions."

Craig was not convinced altruism was the motive for offering him a small fortune. "So I should accept this is as just their way of being magnanimous?" he retorted. "I suppose you would want me to sign some kind of nondisclosure agreement?"

"The subject hasn't been brought up," Pang answered in his soothing timbre. "Know simply that the network board is very disturbed by what has happened to a loyal employee."

Pang's rehearsed tone struck Craig as something foul and rotting inside layers of sanitized cloth.

And Craig was curious about something else. "How about Betty Ann Crawford? Will the network be sending her back to Tennessee with just a thank you and a *don't let the door hit you on the way out?*"

"This may surprise you, Craig, but I was charged yesterday to deliver the winner's cheque of three million dollars to Ms. Crawford. But she said she would not accept it."

Somehow, this did not surprise Craig in the least. If he had learned anything about the intriguing Betty Ann Crawford, it was he had sorrowfully misjudged her.

"So, she's not interested in the money after all?"

"No," Pang said. "Instead, she legally signed the entire amount over to Brent Price and his mother."

Craig shook his head with a laugh. "How I wish Gerald Agee was there to have seen it!" He couldn't help but smirk at the irony of it all. "But I suppose the nondisclosure clauses she signed before filming might be meaningless now that the feds are involved, huh?"

Pang closed the briefcase and got to his feet. His voice was amicable as he said, "Perhaps such clauses wouldn't hold up in federal court. But if Ms. Crawford's actual goal is fame, she would be foolish to use this experience as a vehicle toward that end. The network may see the prudence in taking The Debunker's Challenge off the air, but there are certain benefactors who will not allow the underlying premise of the show to be compromised."

"Premise? Tell me, would that be the premise of sanctimonious reason or the one of fanatical skepticism?"

Pang looked thoughtful. "If I were in your place, Craig, I suppose it is reasonable to construe things under a suspicious light. For the network, it is sufficient to say these benefactors have invested a great deal of time and resources into projects intended to educate people. To help lead the public away from the superstition so inherent in spiritualism, religion, and other beliefs not validated by science. To show them the ignorance of such things."

"In other words," Craig said, "to shame people into believing exactly what these benefactors want them to believe. That, Agee would say, is a technique which has been practiced by institutionalized religion for centuries."

Pang shrugged. "The irony is neither here nor there. My point is these benefactors wield influence over the media. They aren't afraid to use that same media to invalidate any attempt Ms. Crawford may try to exploit from recent events."

Craig shook his head in disgust. "This is the Worldwide Reason Institute you're talking about, right? I know Agee was a disciple, perhaps even a card-carrying member."

Pang smiled. It was a charming smile, though as devoid of warmth as the envelope he'd handed Craig. "I am not at liberty to say."

"You don't have to say it," Craig replied.

Pang asked Craig to extend his condolences to Kesha. And with a thank you, the attorney left.

*\*\*\**

Later that day, after some consideration, Craig took the cheque to the bank. He deposited the money into the joint account he shared with Kesha. When he returned home, Heather was up, and Kesha just getting back from school. He sat them both down in the dining room and told them about Pang's visit -at least the part about him bringing the cheque. Then, he showed them the receipt for the bank deposit.

Craig stood by Kesha's side as she looked at it. She shook her head incredulously and passed it over to Heather to see.

"My god, Craig!" Kesha said. "This is so, so generous." She swallowed. "But it feels wrong somehow to accept such an amount. Our little brother was so gruesomely…" Her voice trailed away, and she wept into her hands.

Craig put an arm around her shoulders. "Kristophe's worth is priceless, sis. There isn't enough money in the universe to make up for what Agee took away." He remembered, with bitterness, the earlier conversation with Pang and said, "I suspect that among the network's executives are those who knew or at least suspected Agee's inclinations. They will never come forward, of course. But, if, as I suspect, it pains them to hand over some of their precious money in the hopes of making amends, then so be it. Let it pain them now. Let it pain them forever."

Kesha nodded her head silently. As Craig rubbed her shoulders, he caught the expression on Heather's face as she inspected the deposit receipt. A deep wrinkle stitched her brow.

"Indeed, let it pain them," she said.

*\*\*\**

That evening, while Craig dried the supper dishes and

Heather washed, he noticed how distracted she seemed.

"Heather, you've been so quiet. Are you okay?"

Her mouth pursed while she scrubbed the plate in her hand. "You didn't say it to Kesha, but I suspect the Worldwide Reason Institute has something to do with that money."

"I suspect, too," he confessed. "Though Pang would not confirm it one way or the other."

"Aren't you afraid they might look on your acceptance of that money as an indication you're just going to remain another industry yes-man for their almighty causes?"

Craig shook his head. "They can think whatever they want. But I have absolutely no desire to be further associated with them or their colluding network."

"I know."

"I have to tell you, though," he said, "I strongly believe that one or all of the network heads knew what Agee was about."

Heather placed a hand on the small of her back. As she massaged the area, she said, "It wouldn't surprise me if they did. Not that they'd ever come out and admit it. Oh, Craig, do be careful. If you ever write a book or make a film about what happened...I dread to think what the WRI would do!"

"Sweet Heather, you worry way more than what's good for you. Don't think about the WRI or the network. Instead, how about we talk about that property in Elk City? We can purchase that out right now, you know?"

"Is that something Kesha would want to do?"

"We will ask her, certainly. Not that I'm interested in buying anything more than that property. I want Kesha to have the rest of the money."

Heather inhaled deeply. "Look, Craig, I have spent a lot of time here lately. I know you and Kesha would probably appreciate some time alone."

"Don't be ridiculous," he corrected her. "I like that you

are here. And Kesha likes you. Stay, please?"

"Are you sure?"

"Absolutely. So please say you'll stay? Unless you'd be more comfortable back at your own place, of course."

"No, I wouldn't," she said, smiling. "The selfish truth is I'd rather be here."

Craig was delighted to see her smile. He was about to suggest they go check out the realtor's website again when Kesha walked into the kitchen. Her eyes were wide and gleamed with an emotion Craig couldn't read.

"Craig…"

He grabbed the small linen towel from the drainer and dried his hands. "Is something wrong, Kesh?"

She pointed over her shoulder. "The local news. They just reported it on television."

"What?"

Her lips spread into a weepy, radiant smile. "About an hour ago, Gerald Agee was found in his cell. The sicko hung himself. He's dead, Craig."

Craig felt the towel fall from his hands.

\*\*\*

In less than twelve hours, the circumstances surrounding the former host's death hit the media. The official report was Agee had been found by a federal corrections officer who had discovered him hanging from the upper bunk of a cell bed. According to the known details, Agee had ripped the welting out of the old pillow on his bed, then tied one end to the mattress frame and used the other end as a noose. Agee had left no suicide note, and his attorney had already proclaimed his client was adamantly helping to prepare for his legal battles. The same attorney was calling for an investigation into the facility and every officer who had been on duty on Agee's floor during the believed time of death. And while it seemed Agee had simply taken the coward's way out, his fans were already weaving together a conspiracy theory. They claimed he had been singled out for psychological torment by the correctional officers simply because he was an outspoken atheist. This torment, they insisted, had led him to end his life.

Craig would never be convinced Agee had committed suicide. Neither did he believe Agee had been killed off over some bias toward his beliefs. There were shadowy entities at work, yes, ones that worked under the protective umbrella of the powerful Worldwide Reason Institute. But Craig did not expect Agee's defenders to actually come out and accuse the WRI of involvement. The organization was a sacred cow for every self-respecting skeptic across the globe.

On the other hand, Craig anticipated the public fascination with Agee's death and the charges for which he'd never stand trial to be fully exploited. The story was ripe fodder for crime books, conspiracy videos, and documentaries. He also knew Agee's cultish admirers would do their best to ennoble his reputation for future generations. At some point, they'd succeed in turning Agee into a martyr, and Brent Price and his other victims would be mere footnotes in their narratives.

In the meantime, authorities continued their search for the victims Betty Ann had said were to be found in other states.

One day, Eileen Robards dropped by Craig's home. She informed him that the local authorities and CBI were done questioning Betty Ann. The FBI might have questions for her in the future, Robards disclosed, but for the present, the young woman was free to return to Tennessee.

Craig realized he should pay a visit to the young woman before she left. He was apprehensive to think how she might react to seeing him. Surely, she knew the awful things he had, for a time, believed about her. He had insinuated the worst about Betty Ann's relationship with Fred Wagoner.

He had pegged her as a charlatan. He had blamed her for his visions. He had threatened her over the phone.

But in the end, the need to apologize and offer Betty Ann a thank you was greater than his remorse.

\*\*\*

Near sunset of the following day, Craig made the drive out to the Relax-o-Lodge. The young man who manned the registry told him Ms. Crawford was still booked in room 8. Craig walked out of the office and down the first floor's exterior gallery until he reached the right door. With a steadying breath, he raised his hand to knock.

The door abruptly opened. Betty Ann stood there, dressed in the same clothes she'd worn that first day they'd met: the denim cut-offs, the old *Boston* tee shirt, the sandals with the rhinestone beaded straps, the little seashell pasta dangle at her wrist. The last rays of daylight now splayed over her loose blonde hair, giving it the luster of gold. And if Craig had ever seen eyes as closer to the color of the sky, he could not recall.

For a moment, he was revisited by the near desirous reaction he'd felt seeing her that first time.

"Hello, Craig," she greeted him. "It's good to see you."

Her friendliness was a relief, though Craig had no doubt her psychic abilities had warned her to know he was coming by.

"I should have come by sooner," he said. "How are you?"

She told him she'd never felt better, then asked after him and his sister.

"We are good, thank you. Would it be okay if I came in for a few minutes?"

"Certainly."

She let him in and closed the door. The inn room was dark except for a slit of sunlight peeking between the window curtains. Betty Ann switched on the overhead light, and as Craig's eyes adjusted to the illumination, he was dismayed. Compared to an ordinary motel room, this cheap room was cramped and unsightly, the ceiling stained from water damage. The colors of the striped wallpaper were indefinable for age and wear. The bed itself was very hard looking, the coverlet shoddy. The one dresser appeared to be at least fifty years old. A little round sitting table –its veneer peeling down the legs– stood near the window along with two rickety chairs. A standard room telephone sat on the nightstand, and a television, very banged up, was affixed to the wall, much like those he'd seen in hospital rooms. Craig noticed the bathroom door was shut, and he could only pray it wasn't as uninviting as he imagined. At the window was an air conditioner, which produced a clunky, tortured sound as it ran. Noting the warmth of the room and the musty smell of the air, Craig guessed the fan was the only part of the ancient contraption that still worked.

The single cheerful item in the room was a cut bouquet arrayed in a crystal case standing atop the dresser. The flowers were lovely: brilliantly colored daylilies, purple alliums, shoots of ferns, and a couple of other plants Craig couldn't name.

"Those are lovely, Betty Ann."

"Zane Kraft sent them."

This came as no surprise to Craig. Kraft was a respectable guy, and he had remained his unbiased self all through Betty Ann's challenges.

"That was very thoughtful. Kraft's a decent dude." Craig caught the shy smile that came to Betty Ann's face. "I take it he likes you. Maybe you like him, too?"

"He called to talk."

"Really?" Craig grinned. "He wants to see you again, doesn't he?"

She laughed lightly. "I told him thank you, but no."

Craig knew it wasn't any of his business, so he said nothing more on the subject.

Betty Ann motioned to the table. "Please, Craig, sit."

After they each took a chair, Craig apologized for the condition of the room.

"Betty Ann, I am so sorry I had you put in this god-awful place!"

She made a dismissive gesture. "I've been in worse places. Besides, I am going home in the morning."

"Yeah, I heard the police and those CBI agents are all done talking with you."

"Yes."

Craig's throat felt thick, and he couldn't tell if it was because of the stale air or just the deep remorse for having been so wrong about her.

"Betty Ann," he said, "I want to thank you for what you did. My sister and I owe you more than I can ever say."

"It must have been hell for you and your sister, not knowing what had happened to Kristophe. But I am sorry I felt no choice but to proceed as I did."

"Whatever for?"

"Gerald Agee," she said with a little frown. "I knew all along he was involved with your brother's disappearance. And that of Brent Price. I could have said something earlier."

"It would have done no good, Betty Ann. At that junction, no one would have believed you. Everyone thought you were just a fake...I thought you were a fake. It took the first two challenges for anyone to realize..." Craig's throat tightened with emotion. "To realize you honestly know things other people don't. Things that some of us just hope to never hear."

Betty Ann's gaze turned remote, her face paled with tragic contemplation. "Such an evil man. He hurt so many."

"Please don't blame yourself," Craig implored. "You went about it the smart way. And Gerald Agee had a long run doing what he did. From what the detectives and agents have determined, he started decades ago."

He leaned over the table and clasped one of her hands. "So I thank you, Betty Ann. I owe you a debt that cannot be repaid. But I also want to apologize. I misjudged you. And for this, I am deeply, deeply sorry."

Betty Ann blinked, and the tragic look fled from her face. "I am not hurt by what doubts you had, so please don't dwell on those? Just know I am forever grateful you gave me this chance."

Craig told her that he knew she'd rejected the prize money. He asked her why she would turn it down? And what were her plans for when she got back to Tennessee?

Betty Ann offered a shrug. "We both know there are more important things than money. What I want is to just get back where I am needed. Where I feel loved. As long as we are needed and loved, I think we're where we are supposed to be."

She was right. Craig understood now why Fred Wagoner cared so much about her, why all his old friends felt the same way. Betty Ann was the first genuine medium he'd ever met, perhaps the last one he would ever meet. But she was more than a medium. She was honest and selfless, both qualities sorely lacking in the world.

"I suppose," he said, "that you've heard Agee is dead?"

Betty Ann answered that she had. And though the important thing was Gerald Agee could never hurt anyone else again, Craig's curiosity compelled him to ask, "Was it suicide like they say?"

With a slow shake of her head, Betty Ann answered, "No. Agee had become a liability for his powerful benefactors. But suicide is the *official* story they'll work hard to have the public accept."

"I see. That's kind of what I figured."

He asked if she wanted to get out of the room for a while? "I'll buy you a decent dinner," he suggested. "Show you the sights by night if you'd like? I have a feeling you haven't had much time to do that since coming to California."

"You are sweet, but no," she said. "One of those nice agents is coming early in the morning to drive me to the airport. And besides, I do believe Heather will need you before the night is over."

Craig was perplexed. When, in the next moment, he understood her implication, the hairs on his arms tingled.

"Are you sure?" He grinned at the absurdity of the question. If Betty Ann said it, it had to be true!

She nodded. "You should probably head back home."

"Oh gosh, alright!" He got to his feet and fished for his car keys from his pants pocket. As Betty Ann stood up, he knew with some sadness that this might be the last time he would ever see her. He would always feel indebted to Betty Ann, and as much as this, he truly liked her. Very much so.

"Heather loves you. You know this, right?" Betty Ann said.

The unexpected question took Craig off guard. "That makes me happy to hear," he admitted. "I love Heather. I've loved her for a long time, actually."

"She's afraid to tell you, fearful you will think she clings to you out of fear or loneliness. It isn't true, Craig. She loves you deeply, sincerely."

This conversation was awkward, though he was sure Betty Ann had what she felt was a reason for telling him these things.

"Well, thank you," he said. "And I won't forget. I will tell Heather how I feel as soon as I see her."

Betty Ann beamed. "Good."

For an instant, he considered asking if she'd consider telling his future? But no, even if she had the ability to see into the future, he knew the journey of life couldn't truly be savored if one knew everything that lay ahead.

"I will call you," he told her. "Make sure your flight back to Tennessee went smoothly. And just to talk, if you'd like. I can reach you through Fred Wagoner?"

"I will never be far from Fred's place," she promised. "Now you go, Craig. And kiss that baby for me?"

Craig nodded. He started for the door but paused. And walking back, he embraced her. She did not flinch or push him away; in fact, she hugged him back. Her arms were smooth and cool in his embrace. The fragrance of her skin filled his nostrils with a hint of exotic perfume. Like a combination of roses and sweet peas, it was, and he knew he'd smelled this before, though he couldn't remember where. It didn't matter. For one poignant moment, he wanted nothing more than to luxuriate in that smell, to hold her and never let go. He knew that had they met under different circumstances, perhaps at some other time, another place, it was very possible he could have fallen in love with Betty Ann.

But Heather was the one he knew for certain he loved. As dear as Betty Ann was, as deeply as he respected her and would always be grateful to her, he couldn't envision anything more satisfying than to spend the rest of his life with Heather and her baby.

"I hope you will be happy," he said. "You deserve that."

She whispered in a blithe tone, "I will be now, Craig."

"Goodbye, Betty Ann."

Craig deposited a little kiss on her cheek and left the room. Once he made his way to the end of the gallery, his phone hummed inside his front shirt pocket. He pulled it out and saw it was Kesha's number. He tapped the answer button.

"Hey, sis. What's up?"

"You need to come home, brother," Kesha announced, her voice more buoyant than it had been for days. "Heather's water broke. And I can't get her to leave for the hospital without you."

Craig said he was on his way. Before taking another step, he looked back for a moment at the door of room 8. And with a smile, he walked to his car.

***

*Three weeks later*

Craig set up the first pot of coffee for the day. It was just after eight o'clock in the morning; the sun outside was bright, and the temperature was mild. Kesha had left for class, and Heather was still in bed. Craig vaguely remembered Heather getting up around three a.m. to feed the baby. He was proud of Heather; she was already proving to be a great mom. And little Teagan was adorable in every way a baby should be. As soon as she'd been born Kesha had claimed aunt status. Between his sister and Heather's mom –who visited almost every day– Craig knew it wouldn't be long before Teagan was properly spoiled.

The day after Teagan's birth, Craig had asked Heather to marry him. To his immeasurable joy, she had accepted his proposal. Marriage was not everything he hoped for, either. He told Heather he wanted to adopt Teagan and be her dad in every way. So Heather had engaged an experienced family attorney to track down Thad in Canada. Once Thad was found, she would ask him to release parental rights. Heather and Craig shared the belief the self-absorbed actor would happily relinquish his paternal claims and responsibilities. But even if Thad surprised them and balked at the idea, Craig had no plans to treat Teagan any less than as his own child.

While the coffee brewed, he thought about the previous day. Agent Robards had called to say that the CBI was done with their autopsy and had the official report on Kristophe's cause of death. She filled him in on the grim details of the coroner's findings: traces of a lethal drug cocktail had been found in Kristophe's remains, most likely given to him at some point following his abduction. Craig did not have to ask who had given it to his brother. Robards had also informed him that preparations were being made to have Kristophe's remains transferred to the funeral home of Craig and Kesha's choice. He instructed her they wanted to use the Idyll Gardens Funeral Services as they'd decided to have Kristophe cremated. One day, in the near future, they would take his ashes back to Spruce Grove. It was there, years before, they had all grown up. It was there, too, their parents had been killed in a car accident. Following that loss, Kesha and Craig had released their parents' ashes on the grounds of the little chapel where their mother and father had been married years before. For Kesha and Craig, there was no more fitting place to say their final goodbyes to Kristophe.

　　With the coffee ready, Craig poured himself a cup. He carried it to the dining table, where his computer was set up. He sat down and sipped the hot liquid, and began to pore through the latest deliveries coming through his email server. Most of the items were junk, but he did notice one marked with the subject: *Receipt for your real estate purchase.* He opened it, finding it had been sent from the Elk City real estate agent he'd done business with the day before.

　　The email read: *Mr. Herbert, attached you will find the receipt for your recent purchase of three lots and property on Gold Twain Road. I have also included a copy of my fee, which was included with the purchase. It is advisable you make a hard copy of this document for your records. Another copy will be arriving to you via certified U.S. mail delivery. We thank you for trusting our company with your real estate needs. If I can be of further service or can be of assistance with your family's upcoming move to Idaho, please contact our offices.*

    *Regards, Helen Clark*

    *Clark Family Land & Auction House*

    Craig set his cup down and saved a copy of the email to a file. He would have this printed off later, but at the moment, he just looked forward to telling Heather about the purchase. It was the property she had found, and the future looked very promising for the studio they dreamed about. They would build it right there in Idaho, something he was sure Kesha would be delighted about. They would be all the closer to Spruce Grove and their family roots, just as his sister wanted. Craig also thought it would be a much better place for little Teagan to grow up. It was removed from Hollywood and the studio that reminded them so much of Gerald Agee.

    "Craig?"

    He looked up to see Heather standing at the end of the hallway. She was still wearing her nightshirt, her hair tousled in a way he found very enticing.

    "Good morning. Want some coffee?"

    She stepped to him, covering a yawn as she did so. When it was over, she said drowsily, "Maybe in a few minutes."

    Craig slipped his arms around her waist and gave her a gentle squeeze. "I love you."

    She cupped his face between her hands and kissed the tip of his nose. "I love you, too. So very much."

    "I expected you to sleep a little longer."

    A little scrunch crinkled her brow. "About that," she said, "I was awakened by a phone call from my mom. She sent something you need to look at."

    "Okay. What is it?"

    She shook her head. "I'd rather just show you."

    Craig nodded and followed her down the hall to his bedroom, or actually what he was now calling *their* bedroom.

Little Teagan's bassinet stood by the wall close to the side of the bed where Heather slept. Diapers and other infant essentials draped the top of Craig's dresser.

He noticed the baby appeared to be asleep in the bassinet.

"Is Teaggie okay?"

"She's fine. Sleeping good." Heather gestured to her laptop, which she'd opened on top of the unmade bed. Her phone lay on top of her pillow. "Sit down, and I'll show you."

They crawled onto the mattress. Craig eyed the laptop; it was on, though the screen saver with its scenery of exotic fish swam busily across the display.

"Like I said, my mom called," Heather explained. "She had been woke up herself by a call from Uncle Fred."

"Uncle Fred? Is he alright?"

"Yeah, he's alright," she said. "But he told Mom about something that broke headlines over his local news channel last night. It was uploaded in a video on their website. Uncle Fred said we would want to see it. And that you, in particular, would want to see it."

"Me?"

"Yeah."

Craig didn't understand. "And it's just local news from Tennessee?"

There was an uncertain strain in Heather's voice, "It is, yes. But it's hard to explain. Let me just pull it up, and you can see for yourself?"

He watched as she tapped the keyboard's Enter button. A flash of light scattered the fish to reveal a webpage. At the top was a header that read *WIJI Local News & Weather*. Below this was a standard rectangular navigational menu, and inches beneath this, the computer's pointing finger cursor rested over a headline in bold print:

FBI CONFIRMS IDENTITY IN 42-YEAR-OLD

MISSING PERSONS CASE

Heather scrolled down to a video embedded at the top of the article. She prompted the cursor, and the video commenced to play.

A segment opened during a broadcast of a television news report. A young male anchor sat behind the news desk while the WIJI logo appeared in the green screen backdrop. Craig noticed the headlines moving across the bottom of the screen were all about sports events from Sullivan County, Tennessee. He remembered this was the county Fred Wagoner lived in.

The audio began as the anchor now spoke: "The county coroner's office has identified human remains retrieved earlier this week by agents with the Federal Bureau of Investigation. As viewers may remember, the search was recently commenced on Squirrel Hollow Road near Blountville, following a tip the FBI acted on in regard to a nationwide investigation of exploited children. Surprisingly, the investigation and an accompanying coroner's report have brought to close a local missing persons case that began in nineteen-seventy nine."

A shiver whispered up Craig's spine. "That's near your uncle's senior center, right?"

Heather nodded. At that moment, an image popped up on the green screen at the anchor's shoulder. It was a photo of a child. He was an attractive white boy with glossy auburn hair. Craig had no idea who the boy was, though he couldn't help but feel there was something familiar about his expressive eyes.

"Mason Goforth," the anchor addressed his audience, "was only six years old when he was reported missing on August 15, 1979, by Cayo Fitzsimmons, the now-deceased fiancé of the boy's half-sister. FBI investigators have confirmed Mason was one of the children thought to have been assaulted and murdered by suspected child molester Gerald Agee. Found alongside Mason Goforth's remains were those of his half-sister, who had also been reported missing at the time of Mason's disappearance. The coroner's report confirms young Mason suffered pre-mortem skull injuries prior to partial burial in a heavily scrub-covered local lot. This lot lies behind a local venue previously used to host traveling carnivals and other entertainment shows."

The photo of the boy disappeared, replaced by another photo. Mason was pictured in this one as well. It apparently had been taken in a wooded area, and the little boy stood in front of a taller figure. Her arms were laced lovingly around his shoulders, and her golden hair cascaded against his shoulder. The two of them beamed for the unknown photographer. As the studio camera zoomed in on their features, Craig's blood froze.

The anchor continued, "The half-sister sister, twenty-year-old Betty Ann Crawford, suffered two gunshots to the head. She and Mason had moved to the Tricities from Hawkins County shortly following their parents' deaths three years earlier. Ms. Crawford was known locally as a holistic healer and was young Mason's legal custodian. The two left behind no known living family members."

Craig felt Heather's fingertips on his arm. Her voice trembled as she asked, "Do you think Uncle Fred knew? Or his friends at the seniors center?"

"I don't know," he answered. "I really do not know."

Through the tears clouding his vision, Craig knew the answer was irrelevant. He only knew he would never again see Betty Ann in this lifetime. She had fulfilled her reason for reaching out to Fred Wagoner. She had succeeded in getting an invitation to be on The Debunker's Challenge. She had revealed what had befallen Kristophe and confronted the man who had hurt so many. She had even stayed long enough to help the authorities locate Agee's other victims. And she'd returned to that place she had alluded to while her blue eyes shone sweetly and the pasta bracelet dangled from her wrist. It was where she felt forever needed and loved, the place she was supposed to be.

*THE END*

Beth Perry has written extensively on the subjects of folklore, legends, and the paranormal for books and other media. One of her favorite pastimes is exchanging "spooky" stories around a cozy winter's fire with her family members. She attended ETSU and presently resides in Eastern Tennessee. Although she has written Romance professionally under a pseudonym, she is currently enjoying creating darker fiction for readers.

www.ingramcontent.com/pod-product-compliance
Lightning Source LLC
Chambersburg PA
CBHW031352170626
46807CB00002B/933